UNDULY SWORN

A NOVEL

TERRENCE BROTHERS

Library of Congress Cataloging-in-Publication Data is available upon request.

Paperback ISBN 978-1-7337303-0-3
Ebook ISBN 978-1-7337303-1-0

Cover design by Arcane Book Covers
Printed in USA

CHAPTER 1

Summer Sinclair, a fabulous fifty-year-old wife, mother, and professional business owner did whatever it took to be successful. She understood the value and the power of the all-purpose gem hovering above her inner thighs, of which she used to her advantage every chance she got. She was an empirical woman who knew the virtue of patience, a rewarding trait that most people lacked.

She was of the opinion that *perfection* couldn't and shouldn't be rushed—if she could master the discipline to sit back and wait, everything she desired would come to her, eventually. However, mustering and maintaining that level of discipline was easier said than done, and just like all humans, sometimes impatience got the best of her. A speedy recovery from a mishap is ideal, but they can sometimes be fatal, depending on the circumstances.

What Summer Sinclair didn't understand was that everything had a price, and that price sometimes is not worth it—something she learned the hard way. Not that it was her preference, but for the decision she made, there was no recourse.

Summer, however, was pragmatic and simply the truth. Ideally she was as real as they come—a woman who talked the talk and walked the walk. Her background was Romanian, although she knew nothing about Romania or its culture, besides the fact that her ancestors and parents were gypsies.

She believed the true essence of life was about give and take—even if it meant being a whore and a slut at times, to her, if it was done with taste, it was okay.

"Fuck!" she said as soon as her eyes opened. She scrambled to get out of bed, noticing how late it was. She reached for the alarm clock and slung it hard against the wall, and watched as it broke into little pieces.

Getting a quick workout or eating breakfast was out of the question; she showered and scurried to get dressed, hating that her day was already off to a bad start. She planned to stop at a deli near the courthouse right after court, and hoped to squeeze in a workout if her schedule permitted, even if it meant kicking off her heels and doing crunches in the center of her office floor. She liked doing everything at her leisure, and took great pride in being punctual. Being rushed to do anything was one thing she hated. It wasn't the way she liked to operate because her entire day would be off track.

She climbed behind the wheel of her Lexus and quickly pulled the door shut as the engine sprung to life. The high-performance tires screeched a bit as she backed out of the driveway and into the street. Her neighbor and best friend Kerry threw up a wave from her yard as she watered her plants.

Normally she'd have time to stop and chat a bit, but not today. Instead of waving back, she gave her friend a honk as her car shot forward, her only concern was making it to court in time. *I'll call her later* she said to herself.

Although Kerry was a housewife, the two women came from symmetrical families, but opposite backgrounds. The Gaines were black; the Sinclairs white, but regardless of that, their husbands and daughters were also close, best friends in fact. Kerry's husband Kevin was a lieutenant for the Las Vegas Metropolitan Police Department. Summer's husband Matt was a paramedic. Their daughters Ke'Auna and Heather, both fourteen, attended Alexander Shaw High School, sharing some of the same classes—both dreamed of being nurses when they grew up. They lived in The Oceanblue Estates, a neighborhood that was predominately white, except for the Gaines and one other family. Everyone seemed to get along well, or at least, pretended to.

Summer reached the corner of Beech Family Street and accessed Google Maps on her cell phone. She had to be in court in twenty minutes, but lived thirty minutes away from the courthouse. She hoped to shave off time from her travels without being pulled over and ticketed for speeding, but getting a ticket was the least of her worries. However, she wanted to reach her destination without incident.

Life in Clark County was shaping up nicely for her. Her health was good; her family was stable and safe; and her career as a criminal defense lawyer in Las Vegas had finally blossomed. She'd been a public defender for the juvenile system for seven years, and she loved it, but she liked the adult system a lot more. Mainly because it was more lucrative and the hours were as flexible as she needed them to be, except for when it came time for her to be in court. Having her own firm was the most rewarding, but the upkeep was a shitload of work—it was the main contributor to her salary increase, but it wasn't the only reason she was raking in dough.

She vowed to forever be grateful to the juvenile system for starting her career. It's where she honed her craft, and learned hands-on how the system worked—it took her a little over a year to learn the ropes. Most cases were the same run-of-the-mill, only a handful presented different challenges, depending on the presiding judge and the district attorney that was handling it. Each day often came with its own challenges, but to be a good attorney, one had to be able to rise to the occasion, treading through the grit and grind of law that contradicts itself, and the countless legal maneuvers, is what separated a good lawyer from a bad one. Summer Sinclair was one of the best.

After three years of being a private attorney, her courtroom record revealed a helluva lot more wins than losses; she was sought after by more and more clients because of her fearlessness to go directly at the throats of all the ruthless cold-hearted judges and prosecutors she came across, which turned out to be plenty, in a relentless legal game of tug of war—a game that seemed to be non-stop.

Without trying she'd worked herself into the big league where she could no longer distinguish an ally from an enemy.

In the three years she'd been in private practice, she earned nearly three times more cash than she had in the seven years she'd been a juvenile public defender. Things were really looking great for her, but for how long?

She was fully aware that, whether good or bad, nothing lasts forever—not even life itself. Mrs. Sinclair was about to be tested beyond all boundaries. The costs of losing could cost her everything—she could lose her life, as well as those she called her family.

She entered Judge Dan Silva's courtroom nonchalantly, but filled with confidence, just as he was calling her case, dressed casual but sexy, in a pair of tight-fitted white slacks that couldn't conceal the prominent W-shape of her crotch, slightly covered by a black-knitted sweater that clasped her shapely hips. A loose curl of jet-black hair dangled stylishly down the left side of her face while the rest of her hair was swooped to one side, hanging over her shoulder, covering one of her breasts.

She strode with elegance to the defense table, wearing black suede red-bottom stilettos, strutting in them with ease as if she was wearing a pair of Nike tennis shoes, filling the air surrounding her with Chanel Gabrielle perfume.

She laid a thin beige folder on the top of the defense table and flipped it open. She put on her fancy black-framed reading glasses and skimmed over some notes, ignoring everyone inside the courtroom, as if she was alone.

"Mrs. Sinclair, you're bordering on contempt," the judge said mild-mannered as everyone inside the courtroom stared at her. "We're on the court's time, not yours," he reminded her.

"Oh, I'm sorry, judge," she said when she looked up. "I didn't have time to go over my notes this morning. The batteries literally died in my alarm clock so I woke up late. I indulge the court and ask for its forgiveness. I didn't mean to show up so unprepared. Again, I ask for your indulgence, Your Honor."

"Meet me in my chambers in twenty minutes, counselor. It seems I need to personally give you a list of the rules of this court. Apparently your memory has failed you."

"If you say so, judge," Mrs. Sinclair replied, feeling somewhat embarrassed by the public scolding. She had already offered her apologies, so she didn't understand what the judge was doing. "I'll be in your chambers in twenty minutes, Your Honor."

"Please do," Judge Silva replied. "This matter is to address the motion to lower the bail of your absentee client Raymar Ray. Does the state have anything to say?"

"The state does, Your Honor," a pudgy district attorney said without standing. "We strongly oppose the reduction of bail. We feel that the defendant is a serious flight risk. He has very strong ties to Northern California. If he flees the state, we may never find him."

"Motion requesting reduction of bail is hereby denied," snarled the judge as he slammed his gavel. Twenty minutes later they were alone in his chamber.

"Dan, what the fuck was that?" Attorney Sinclair asked as she stood in the middle of the floor with one hand on her hip.

"A show."

"A show for what?"

"I don't know. I guess I just felt like giving you a hard time," he said as he leaned against his desk. "Don't take it personal, Summer. Come here."

She approached him and stood between his legs with her thigh against his crotch, then grazed his forehead with her thumb and spoke softly, "A hard time, huh? You must have forgotten that two can play that game, remember that the next time your dick gets hard," she said as she turned away from him and headed toward the door, intentionally pushing out her ass as she neared it.

"I don't get a treat?" asked Judge Silva.

"A treat for what? You haven't earned a treat. Aren't you the one who denied my motion?"

"Re-file it today or tomorrow and I'll grant it."

"Let's not discuss treats until that happens," she said flatly. "Until then, have fun jacking off. I'm sure it wouldn't be the first time you've done it."

The motion for reduction of bail was re-filed the following day, and immediately granted by Judge Silva. He refuted the State's argument that Raymar Ray was a flight risk. Mr. Ray was released on bail later that evening—it wasn't long before he disappeared.

CHAPTER 2

The movie based on actual events on the Lifetime Network ended at 6PM. It was Kerry's turn to keep Heather at her house for the night so that her mommy and daddy could get some private time. It was a tradition their families adopted years earlier when the girls were eight, something both families took turns doing once or twice a month.

The evening was young and shaping up to be a beautiful one. Kerry was in the midst of trying to figure out what they could do next when her daughter Ke'Auna came up with an idea," Mom, can we play dress up?"

"We played dress up last time, honey. How about we go out and get some ice cream?" her mom suggested.

"I don't want ice cream though. Neither does Heather," Ke'Auna pouted, acting more like an adolescent than a teenager, trying to play on her mom's weakness so she could get her way.

"How would you know when you haven't asked her?" her mom retorted. "Heather, I'm going to let you be the tie-breaker. Do we go out for ice cream or play dress up? You know you guys just played dress up a few weeks ago."

"Let's play it again. I like playing dress up," replied Heather. She really had a craving for raspberry sherbet, but chose to play dress up again to not upset her friend.

"Dress up it is then," Kerry said as she stood up to stretch, then grabbed her iPhone from the coffee table. "Would it be okay if we just do clothes and shoes but no makeup?"

"That's fine with me. I don't feel like getting my face all yucky this time anyway," said Ke'Auna. "I do like lipstick though. Heather, what do you think?"

"I'm fine with just clothes and shoes."

"Good," Kerry said quickly. "Y'all already know where everything is at so go ahead and pick out your costumes and let me see what y'all got."

Both girls ran down the hallway to Kerry's bedroom. For the purpose of the game, Kerry kept a bunch of old-school clothes stored in the back of her closet that she no longer wore, someone on the outside looking in might have easily mistaken her for a hoarder.

Kerry loved hanging out with the girls. It gave her something to do besides keep house, at times she even considered getting a part time job to pass the time, but she preferred hanging out with the girls because it gave her a chance to keep her eye on them, as well as helped her stay youthful—she treated them equally as if she'd birthed them both.

She sat on the sofa and grew impatient as she waited for the girls to exit her bedroom. She knew they would more than likely wear a costume that they'd worn before, but still, she enjoyed judging who was the best dressed, and offered tips on being classy whenever she could. To her, it was a huge difference between classy and trashy, and she wanted to be sure that the girls got it right. It was all in the name of fun. It gave the girls a chance to express their sense of fashion, the fact that they were all around the same size, was a bonus.

"Mrs. Gaines, are you ready?" Heather said from the back of the hall-way.

"I'm ready, sweetie. Come on out," replied Kerry.

Heather came down the hallway, wearing a long curly black wig that was pulled back in a bun; a pair of high heels that were high, but not too high, and a long red dress that came past her knees. She went out of her way and made sure to cover every part of her body—she knew the lone judge would be impressed.

Kerry was in awe as she observed who she considered to be her second daughter, and as many times as they'd played the game, she hadn't realized the young teen had such good taste. "You look so beautiful, Heather. Great job. I'm so proud of you. Your mom would be proud too," she said with admiration. "That's exactly how I dress when I dress up. Matter of fact, I might put that on tomorrow now that I see how good it looks on you." She gave Heather a smile while snapping head-to-toe pictures with her smartphone.

"Are you ready for me, mom?" Ke'Auna said from the bedroom doorway, clearly excited and anxious to make her debut.

"Come on, baby. Let mama see what you're workin' with," she said, still holding up her phone.

Ke'Auna came strutting down the hallway like it was the red carpet, and nearly tripped. The heels she chose to wear were too high for her.

Kerry's mouth dropped as soon as she saw her daughter. Her phone fell to the floor as she struggled for words. "Ke'Auna, what are you wearing? What are you doing?"

The fourteen-year-old came into the living room and stood next to Heather. She had on an all-black wig with its straight hair spiraled down the center of her back; some ginormous see-through high heels; a pair of wide pink suspenders she used to cover her nipples because she wore no bra; and a pair of pink g-string panties that cut deeply into her front and back crevices, the tight straps of the suspenders made sure of it.

"Baby, what's going on?" her mom asked with a pained look on her face.

Ke'Auna looked at Heather and realized that their idea of a joke was a big mistake. "Mom, I didn't mean to shock you. I'm sorry."

"Girl, what is this? Go in there and take that shit off! Go take it off right now!"

Ke'Auna did as she was told. Her best friend quickly followed suit. She didn't want to be left alone with a woman who was clearly angry. They returned to the living room after about ten minutes, and immediately sensed that the atmosphere had changed.

Kerry nodded her head slowly as she stared at her daughter who was fidgeting with her hair, her best friend uncomfortably standing beside her. "What in the world just happened? For real, baby? You gotta explain to mama what's going on."

It was an awkward moment for the fourteen-year-old. She stood there unable to say anything, looking back and forth between her mom and the floor, a sense of relief flashing across her face when Heather stepped up and spoke for her.

"Mrs. Gaines, it wasn't our intentions to upset you or disrespect you if that's what you feel, but Ke'Auna and I thought it would be a good idea to play a joke on you."

"What kind of hoochie joke was that? How the hell was it a joke with her coming in here basically naked, looking like a prostitute? Ke'Auna and I both know she wasn't raised like that, and neither were you."

"Mom, she was dressed like you and I was dressed like Mrs. Sinclair. We thought you'd recognize it and laugh as soon as you saw us. I'm sorry I was wrong; I won't do it again."

Kerry sighed as she reached down to retrieve her phone from the floor, then stood up and tightly embraced her daughter, "I'm sorry too, baby. I apologize if I overreacted," she said as she stretched out an arm to include Heather.

Smiling, she added, "Just for the record, Summer doesn't dress like that. That girl finesse everything she puts on. That's why she works out so much. She makes the clothes look good, not the other way around."

"If you say so," said Heather as she hugged Ke'Auna. She was glad everything was back to normal. She didn't want tension between mother and daughter—she thought of them both as an extension of her family.

Kerry thought it was a perfect time to change the subject after seeing the smiles on the teenagers' faces. "Girls, it's only 6:40. It's still quite early, so how 'bout we go out and get some ice cream?"

"Can we get some sherbet?" asked Heather.

"Child we can get whatever you want. I just want some ice cream. I honestly don't care what kind it is," Kerry said as she stretched again. "What are your thoughts, Ke'Auna?"

"I'm ready when you are."

"Let's hit it then," Kerry said as she scooped her keys from the coffee table.

As soon as they were inside her truck, Kerry sent a text message to both Kevin and Summer, letting them know that she and the girls were stepping out for a while, she didn't want anyone to be worried about them.

They arrived at Coldstone Ice Cream Parlor a few blocks away, and began quenching their craving of refreshing ice cream.

Kerry watched her daughter and Heather as they licked their ice cream cones, and had a flashback of less than an hour earlier when the girls were playing dress up. She could still visualize Ke'Auna topless, standing in the center of her living room floor, wearing an invasive thong, and couldn't help but wonder if the girls were sexually active?

"I got a question for y'all. Be honest too, okay?"

The two girls gave each other a quick glance, then simultaneously said, "Okay."

"Do y'all have boyfriends?"

"Nooo! You know we aint got no boyfriends," Ke'Auna said, thinking her mom was joking.

"Nope, no boyfriends," added Heather. "We're not interested and don't have time. We're both too busy trying to become nurses."

"So that means you're both still virgins?" Kerry asked with her brows raised, looking back and forth between the two girls.

"Of course," said Heather. "I'll probably be that until I die."

"Me too," said Ke'Auna.

Relieved to learn that the girls were virgins, and not yet interested in boys, Kerry swiped her forehead with her hand and expressed praise, "Whew! I'm so grateful to hear that. I damn near had a heart attack just thinking about it."

They all laughed.

"You don't have to worry about that, Mrs. Gaines," Heather assured her. "Ke'Auna and I are some good girls."

"I know, baby. It's just something that all parents fear."

"Well, you should feel lucky that you don't have to," said Ke'Auna. "Heather and I have made a pact to not have sex until we're married."

"Thank God," said Kerry. "Music to my ears. As your mother I want to ask when and why this pact came about, but right now, I'm not going to even worry about it. I'm just glad you're still untouched."

"I plan to stay that way until I'm married," Ke'Auna assured her.

"Me and her both," added Heather.

"Good. I'm elated," Kerry told them.

They finished their ice cream and went home. Minus a few small bumps in the road, it turned out to be a terrific evening.

The girls went to bed after a hot shower. The topic of their game of dress up never resurfaced, but that doesn't mean Kerry didn't think about it.

She stayed up a while to greet her husband when he got off work. His shift was supposed to end at 8PM, but since his colleague had called and said he was running late, his shift didn't end until 9:30.

Except for his days off, it was really the only time she got to spend with him. When he finally came home, they showered and made love quietly when they hit the sack.

CHAPTER 3

For Lieutenant Kevin Gaines, the morning started no different than any other, except for the fact that it was Friday—the end of a long work-week—the time everyone began preparing to switch over to weekend mode, but in reality, it wouldn't become official for him until clock out time.

He breezed through the light traffic, riding down the stretch of Rainbow Boulevard, arm resting on the window ledge of his patrol cruiser. It was exactly 10:06 when the alarming call came over the radio. An armed robbery was in progress at a Moneytree on Warm Springs and Rainbow and, Lieutenant Kevin Gaines, was less than a block away.

"Copy, I'm en route. I'll be on scene in approximately one minute," he said to the dispatcher. "Is there any description of the perpetrators?"

"Um, it's reported to be a lone assailant. White male; twentyish; wearing dark-colored jeans, either blue or black, with a red bandana around his neck. That's the only description I can provide at this time."

"Copy that. I'm on scene and believe I just spotted the described subject," said Lieutenant Gaines as he stopped at a distance from a man he perceived to be armed and dangerous. He sprung from his cruiser and kneeled inside the driver's door, and began barking orders over his loudspeaker, "YOU IN THE RED BANDANA, LET ME SEE YOUR HANDS!"

The subject ignored the command and kept walking eastward, an opening at the end of the building was fifteen to twenty feet away.

"I REPEAT, SHOW ME YOUR HANDS!"

The subject stopped in his tracks and stared in his direction, then began laughing hysterically as he came toward him, his hands hidden behind his back the entire time. "I'm sorry officer, were you talking to me?" the man said as if he was deranged.

"Sir, stop right where you are and let me see your hands," the lieutenant yelled as he drew his weapon. "Sir, please remove your hands from behind your back, and place them above your head where I can see them!"

"Fuck you officer…I GOT A GUN!" he screamed suddenly while shifting his body, then slung his arms in front of him as if he was aiming a weapon.

As soon as backup patrol cars rounded the corner and stormed the parking lot, all they saw was the body of the potential-robbery suspect hitting the ground while Lieutenant Gaines approached him, still aiming his weapon.

"SHOTS FIRED! SHOTS FIRED!" one of the officers yelled as he leapt from his cruiser, his radio just a few inches away from his mouth. "Suspect down. We need medical assistance!" He watched as Lieutenant Gaines knelt beside the suspect to check his pulse, then gave a nod, indicating there was no sign of life.

"First Responders are en route," the officer said as he stared at the deceased. "The coroner as well."

Lieutenant Kevin Gaines stood hovering over the deceased with his head bowed—he was distraught and in disbelief about what had taken place. He desperately wished that there was some kind of way he could turn back the hands of time and change the outcome, but because his own safety had been jeopardized, he knew he only responded the way he'd been trained—desperate times called for desperate measures—his instincts told him, *it's him or me!* He knew he'd done exactly what he was supposed to, and because of his ability to make such rational and not rash split-second decisions, the only reward he wanted was to return home to his family, and he wanted to do so in one piece.

In the twenty-five years he'd been in law enforcement, not once had he ever had to discharge his service weapon in the line of duty—the fact that he'd actually shot and killed a man was a hard pill to swallow, especially for it to have been a man who appeared as though he had just begun life.

"What happened, lieutenant?" another officer asked while several officers swarmed the area.

Lieutenant Gaines turned his head and vomited, clearly struggling to stomach the thought of having killed someone. "He made me shoot him," he managed to say.

"How?"

"He said he had a gun and took a stance as if he were going to shoot me."

"I don't see any guns, lieutenant," the officer said.

"He was holding something," the lieutenant said as he looked around. "The man shouted that he had a gun. I saw no other alternative, I had to shoot him."

"Well, I don't see any gun, lieutenant. Do you?"

Lieutenant Gaines found himself getting upset at the officer's tone of voice, he felt as though he was being interrogated. "I had no choice but to shoot him, officer," he said respectfully.

"We've bagged and tagged a cell phone that I believe was his. It was lying on the ground about fifteen feet away from his body, but no weapon was recovered, or anything that resembled one. If it was a suicide-by-cop as you're hinting toward, the burden to prove it is on you."

"It happened so fast. I just reacted," said Lieutenant Gaines. "Maybe it was a phone, shit, I don't know."

"So you're unsure whether or not it was a gun or a phone?" asked another officer.

"He screamed it was a gun, then gestured like he was about to shoot, so what was I to think," he said. "I couldn't exactly wait to inspect the object to see if it was really what he said it was, but I knew for a fact that he was holding something."

"Bad call, lieutenant. You just killed an unarmed man; looks to me like you need more training," said a third officer who hadn't been on the force for a year yet.

Before the lieutenant could respond, the captain appeared and pulled him aside, stating he needed to have a word with him, just as the paramedics arrived on scene, "Everyone back up and let medical personnel do their job!" the captain yelled in a commanding voice. The surrounding officers complied and backed up in unison.

Lieutenant Gaines lowered his head once he saw his friend Matthew was not with the group of paramedics who'd arrived on scene. He was shaken and in need of support, he still couldn't believe he'd ended a life. Taking a human being's life was a lot to bear; he fought hard not to cry at the sight of his captain.

Captain McElroy returned to his side after clearing a path for medical personnel, his conduct showed he had a lot of experience, "Lieutenant, I'm going to need you to write out a detailed statement. Chief Dunlap is already all over this, we needed your statement yesterday."

"Captain, he told me he had a gun, then motioned real quick like he was going to shoot me. If he hadn't done that I wouldn't have shot him," explained the lieutenant. "It happened so fast. I vaguely recall pulling the trigger, but he had something in his hand that I thought was a gun."

"Did you activate your body and dash-cam?" the captain asked.

"No, didn't think I'd need to," he stated solemnly.

"Big mistake, lieutenant," replied the captain. "With so many officer-involved shootings in the past year or two, utilizing your cameras should have been one of the first things you thought of. I can tell you right now it's not looking good. Hopefully something that can help you will surface or reveal itself at some point during the investigation."

"What took so long for backup to arrive?"

"I'm asking the questions, lieutenant, not you," the captain told him. "Get in your squad car and go straight to the station. I need you to explain what happened in writing," the captain said then spun off.

Lieutenant Gaines was stunned, but did exactly as his superior had instructed him to. He didn't know why, but he felt like he was being ostracized. He felt far less than a decorated lieutenant who'd been on the job for twenty-five years, he felt as though they were treating him like it was his first day. He struggled to formulate his thoughts. His brain had a hard time making sense of it. It was difficult to fathom.

He'd been on the scene of countless officer-involved shootings during his extensive career, and not once had he witnessed an officer being treated with so much disregard. He was treated as though he'd done something wrong, or at least, that's how they made him feel. The lieutenant had a thought. In mostly all the cases of officer-involved shootings, white cops had killed unarmed black men at an alarming rate, or black cops killed another black, but it was almost unheard of for a black cop to kill a white person, whether armed or not. It was personally the first case he knew of in the city of Las Vegas where a white person had fallen victim to a black officer—a case that was clearly avoidable had the man complied.

This fact alone could have made all the difference in the world; maybe it's where the backlash was coming from?

The decorated lieutenant sent his wife a text message to tell her the news.

He arrived at the station and was met outside by Chief Dunlap. The media frenzy had already begun.

"Chief, can we get a statement of what happened, and is this the officer that did the shooting?" asked a female reporter.

Chief Dunlap sheltered the lieutenant as he whisked him past the cameras and a handful of reporters. He got him safely inside the station then turned to the reporter who'd posed the question, "My officer is the only person right now who knows what took place. I'll provide you with the details when they become available."

"Thanks, chief," the reporter responded, a pretty petite redhead with noticeable dimples.

As soon as Chief Dunlap entered the building, Lieutenant Gaines handed him his badge and service weapon—he knew it was protocol after such unfortunate events.

"Thank you, lieutenant. Hopefully I'll be returning these items back to you soon," he said as he grabbed the hardware. "I'm going to need an intricate statement of what happened this morning. Don't leave out anything. If you farted be sure to include it, am I clear?" he said as they entered his office.

"I know the drill, chief," said Lieutenant Gaines. "Not one iota will be left out."

"Good," replied Chief Dunlap. "So you do understand that you will be placed on administrative leave once I receive your account of events. I hope it appeases every question the press may ask—a barrage of questions from them is inevitable."

"I know, chief, and I'm sorry this happened. If it was at all avoidable, it would have been."

"Apologize to his family, not me. They're the ones you may need to show remorse to," he said coldly. "I expect to have your statement in my hand before the ink dries. You will receive your due process, but will not return to duty until the investigation is complete. I'll leave you now to write out your statement. Internal Affairs will come knocking soon."

Again, Lieutenant Gaines felt alienated as he sat by his lonesome inside the chief's office. His heart heavy, wanting to express his remorse, but felt more like a common criminal than a high-ranked officer. As a lieutenant, not only did he feel he deserved it, but out of courtesy, he should have received a lot more respect—he placed the iPad on his lap and began typing. He made sure not to leave out a single detail.

He slipped deeper and deeper into the abyss of despair, wondering what was happening as the day progressed. The incident was plastered on all the local news channels throughout the day, though none were accurate—protesters were already gathering in the streets of Las Vegas, insisting justice be served, demanding that murder charges be filed against the veteran officer, of whom they accused of senselessly taking the life of an unarmed teenager.

Kerry was tearful when the night fell as she cradled her husband's head as they lie in bed. Her heart went out to him as he cried on and off while lying in her bosom, she had never before seen him in such a feeble state.

She whispered to him that everything was okay and would blow over soon. She had no idea how wrong she was. Things were not about to blow over, and were not okay. In fact, they were about to get worse. Much worse.

CHAPTER 4

A large memorial sprung up overnight at the sight of the shooting. The scene where nineteen-year-old Shane Forbes was gunned down, looked more like a dump-site for a greenhouse, than a strip mall parking lot. Flowers of all sorts had been left in Shane's honor by complete strangers, and carefully placed in the same manner as a floral arrangement. The décor of the brightly colored flowers were simply beautiful, producing a scent that was pleasant to the senses, but beneath it all, was a foul stench. Innocent blood had been shed, according to the press, and the public was calling for justice to be served.

A small group of protesters marched peacefully in front of City Hall in downtown Las Vegas. They also gathered in the street in front of Police Headquarters, requesting charges be filed against Lieutenant Gaines—they didn't seem to understand why he hadn't been arrested.

Chief Dunlap sat comfortably and watched the crowd on a plethora of surveillance monitors from the safety of his office. He had no intentions of arresting or filing charges against his lieutenant. He felt the officer had only did what was necessary, but of course, he had no plans of sharing his personal thoughts with the general public. He knew things could potentially get ugly, even deadly, and prayed that the peaceful protests wasn't the calm before the storm.

He did a press conference that afternoon, and explained to the public that the officer had responded to an armed robbery call and had every right to believe that Shane Forbes was armed. He concluded by saying that the investigation was ongoing, and no charges would be filed at that point of time. He also requested their patience and understanding during the process. The public was simply not trying to hear it. Chief Dunlap was booed as he left the podium; the groups reassembled and continued to protest.

CHAPTER 5

The thick smoke rose rapidly in the dead of night, in a dense area, adjacent to the police department, sparking interest of several people who saw it, more than half of the witnesses were police officers. Phone calls came in back-to-back to the fire department; fire and vandalism calls had more than quadrupled since the shooting death of the nineteen-year-old.

As the flames began to die down, the black smoke turned into a chalky-white smolder, appearing to be packed with harmful chemicals—the first fire truck to arrive approached with caution.

"This appears to be a king or queen sized mattress; it appears to have been set intentionally," the fireman said to the dispatcher.

"Nothing serious?"

"No, nothing serious. We'll have this extinguished in a few minutes. It already looks to be burning itself out," he said with confidence, jumping down the side of the truck, getting a better look at it.

"Copy," the dispatcher said. "I can check this one off as being covered."

"Yes, you may. Have a good day."

"Let's hope so," the dispatcher said. The fire was minor like most of them, but with so many calls in such a short period of time, the workforce was spread thin and caused many to panic.

The powerful water from the hose moved everything around with ease, and just as the firefighter had said, everything was soaked and barely smoking in just under a few minutes. They left the scene headed to their next call.

CHAPTER 6

Not only were the people of the community negatively impacted by the tragedy, but the city itself was suffering, and began automatically separating and segregating themselves—blacks on one side and whites on the other.

Tempers flared at the Sinclair residence as Matt, Kerry and Summer sat inside the family room, watching the news. Kerry found herself at odds with Matt and Summer about the way the local media depicted her husband. She felt their portrayal of Kevin was insensitive and inaccurate, but the Sinclair's perceived it differently.

"Kerry. Kevin is not being singled out," Matt said, trying to sound convincing. "The media does not go out and target anyone just because of their race. They only report the information they're provided with, nothing they say derives from them."

"Are you serious or are you really this blind?" Kerry asked as she took the floor. "Our families have been friends for as long as I can remember, and I had no clue until now that the two of you are racists!"

Summer leapt to her feet with godspeed. "Bullshit, Kerry! How dare you come into my home and call us racists? You're my best friend, how dare you? Maybe we need to re-evaluate our relationship?"

"Maybe we do," Kerry shot back.

"We understand the situation being a stressful one—we get that. We also understand that you need to vent, but my husband and I are just voicing our opinions. If you can't handle it, it's not our fault, but don't come into our home and call us racists. I can't think of anything more disrespectful."

Without thinking, Kerry balled up her fist while looking at Summer. She was tempted to lay hands on her, but was smart enough to know the risk wasn't worth taking, the last thing she needed was to find herself in jail. It angered her even more when Matt stood up and put his arm over his wife's shoulder, she felt like she was being double-teamed. "Do you see those pro-testers strutting up and down the street with those 'White Lives Matter' signs? I'm sure you both know it wouldn't be happening if Kevin were white, right?"

"This could've happened to anyone, Kerry," Matt interjected. "Unfor-tunately it was Kevin's number that came up. I love him; he's my best friend; my brother, and I hate it just as much as you do that he's going through this, but what's happening to him isn't happening just because he's black."

"Some best friend and brother you are, and stop saying that you love him," Kerry told him. "He's a police officer—a lieutenant at that. He's not a thug or some random Joe Blow from the streets. You would think that the police force would support him, or at least try to protect him, and not let the media portray him as someone that they know he's not. If he were a white officer, I'm almost certain this wouldn't be happening. Maybe you have to be black to understand?" she said as tears welled in her eyes.

Matt looked at Summer and shook his head, he knew that talking to Kerry was a lost cause.

Kerry rolled her eyes and shook her head in dismay as she left the family room. As soon as she got inside the hallway, she turned towards Heather's bedroom and yelled for Ke'Auna.

She escorted her daughter out of the house with her arm around her shoulder—the Sinclair family was left speechless.

Kerry said nothing to Ke'Auna as they walked home. She was heated and needed to cool off after reaching an impasse with the Sinclairs; she was grateful her daughter or Heather hadn't witnessed the fallout.

She laid in bed beside her husband when they got home. She did her best to explain everything that was said—he paid careful attention to every word she spoke, and after listening intently, he remained neutral. To him, it sounded like his wife's emotions had gotten the best of her, and he hoped she hadn't caused a rift between the two families. He understood her reasoning for being upset, but he didn't believe in making permanent decisions on temporary problems, he was more than certain things would work themselves out.

CHAPTER 7

Monday mornings were always the toughest, especially when the weekend was brutal, which was definitely the case for Summer Sinclair. She sat rocking back and forth in her comfortable office chair, eating a blueberry muffin, regretting the argument she had with Kerry over the weekend, when her secretary Heidi burst into her office.

"Mrs. Sinclair, your absconding client is on line 1, should I tell him to call you back later?"

Summer nearly bit her tongue when she heard the announcement. She knew exactly which client Heidi was referring to. "I'll take it, are you kidding me?" she said, quickly snatching up a napkin to wipe her mouth. "Raymar, where are you?"

"Oakland," he said nonchalantly, hoping he wasn't making a mistake by calling her.

"Why are you in Oakland, Raymar? You missed a court date last week."

"I know," he stated, offering no remorse. "I gotta be out here with my kids. I can't let those people send me to prison."

Summer wrapped her lips around the straw and drew a slurp from her tea, then wiped the remnants from her mouth and carried on, "A warrant has already been issued for your arrest, you do know that, right?"

"Yeah, I know," he said stoically. "I need to be here with my kids though. I refuse to let them go through what I went through in life. I probably wouldn't be in trouble now if I'd had a father."

She became sympathetic by the way he spoke. It was a sensitive topic but she chose to elaborate, "Do you know him? Your father, that is?"

"Yeah, I know who he is, but he's never been there for me."

"Why?"

"I don't know—only he can answer that," he told her. "He wasn't there for me or my siblings."

"That's sad," said Summer, trying to show sympathy.

"And detrimental, that's why I know I have to be here for mine," added Raymar. "The few times I saw him, he acted like my siblings and I owed him something, as if we got our mom pregnant and had him."

Summer smiled. She'd never quite heard it put like that before, although several of her incarcerated clients spoke about similar experiences. She wished there was something she could do to help, but the most she could do was lend her ear, "Well, thank God you're not like that. Your children has a dad who loves them, at least they'll have a fighting chance."

"My dad did teach me one thing though."

"And, what's that?"

"He taught me how not to be."

"So, what are your plans, Raymar?" asked Summer, changing the subject. "How do you plan to stay free?"

"I don't know, that's why I called you…I just hope it wasn't a mistake?"

"What do you mean?"

"By law, do you have to report that I called you?"

"By law, attorney-client privilege prevents me from doing so, especially if you don't want me to."

"I don't," he said with emphasis.

"Then I won't," said Summer.

"I don't plan to return to Vegas."

"Then don't—it'll better your chances. Coming back here would be a huge mistake," she said. "The warrant isn't going anywhere though. It'll always be there, but if you keep your nose clean, you'll be okay."

"That's what I needed to hear," he told her. "I know as my attorney you can't advise me to run, but what you've said is all I needed to know."

"Stay under the radar and you'll be fine, Raymar. Don't give anyone any reason to run your name."

"Got it."

"Good luck, Raymar."

"Thank you."

She smiled when she hung up the phone. She appreciated the fact that he wanted to be there for his children. *The world would be a much better place if all other dads felt the same way* she thought.

In her heart of hearts, she hoped he would be okay. Even though he was doing something illegal, she was rooting for him.

CHAPTER 8

A week passed since the shooting death of nineteen-year-old Shane Forbes, and the city of Las Vegas was still restless.

Protests continued all over the city. More than a few turned violent and, arrests were made, for charges that ranged from assault to arson—Chief Dunlap was beginning to feel the pressure.

Noticeable tension was building within the police department. White officers began siding with the unfortunate victim, and slowly began separating themselves from black officers on the force, who seemingly didn't understand what was happening or why it was happening, because they, for reasons only they understood, believed Lieutenant Gaines was justified in his actions.

A crowd marched in front of headquarters chanting in unison *'Arrest the criminal!'* and were calling for immediate resignation of Chief Dunlap as they proudly held White Lives Matter signs and other signs that a lot of people thought were offensive, displaying pictures of nooses and hangmen dangling from trees—images that were clearly marked by racism.

No one in their wildest dreams could have ever imagined such a horrific scene playing out in a city as wealthy and famous and friendly as Las Vegas, that seemed to have more in common with the deep south than most people thought—it just took a racially-charged incident to bring it out. Outsiders would have probably wondered if the deep-rooted hatred had been there all along, maybe the natives had just had a clever way of disguising it?

Chief Dunlap watched the protesters on the monitors inside of his office as he sat at his desk with his phone pressed solidly against his ear.

Mayor Kason sat fuming on the other end of the line. The situation he hoped would die down, only seemed to get worse, his goal was to gain control of the simmer before things boiled over. "Chief, maybe you should take a closer look at Lieutenant Gaines' report and see if you can poke a few holes in his story," he said before pausing. "If we can figure out a way to bring charges against him, there's a good chance we can bring some normalcy and order back to this city. Otherwise, it's going to cost the city a lot of money."

The chief of police was at a loss for words. He'd gone over the exposé a thousand times, talked to Lieutenant Gaines several times, asking relevant questions for clarity, and not once did he waver or stray away from his initial story—he knew his lieutenant was telling the truth. "Mayor, I'll look at it again," he said, not feeling good about it, but knew he didn't have any other choice.

"You do that," the mayor told him. "And keep in mind that these demonstrations won't cease unless charges are filed."

Chief Dunlap was stuck between a rock and a hard place. He felt in his gut that his job was in jeopardy, unless he pressed charges against a man he believed was innocent. He began to feel sorry for Lieutenant Gaines. He knew the man didn't deserve what was happening to him, and he wasn't about to jeopardize himself trying to help him. All he could do was wish him luck.

Ke'Auna and Heather walked past each other in the hallway of their school. They hadn't spoken much since the weekend when their families clashed. Even though they hadn't personally gotten into it, their parents' argument was having an impact on them, and it made them uncomfortable when they crossed paths. Some teachers and students noticed how distant the best friends seemed, and was unsure of whose side to take, because they truly enjoyed being around them both. They assumed Ke'Auna's father being in the headlines had something to do with their fallout.

The teens at the school were also beginning to racially divide themselves. It began slowly but surely to look like Jim Crow all over again, and one teacher refused to just stand by and watch. It wasn't in her character to sit back and do nothing.

CHAPTER 9

A huge inferno penetrated the darkness in the middle of the night, propelling a thick shroud of white smoke after straggling protesters set fires in the parking lot of the ginormous state-of-the-art Raiders Stadium—a project that cost the city of Las Vegas nearly two billion to build. Several fire trucks from different fire stations across the valley were called to the site in hopes of saving the beautiful black and silver structure from being destroyed.

A man wearing a swastika that covered the front of his t-shirt boasted to a black fireman that was on scene that, he alone, was responsible for setting the fires. He was immediately placed in handcuffs by one of the officers on scene and told that he was being charged with first-degree arson before being seated in the backseat of a squad car.

The arresting officer studied the ID he took from the suspect and learned the man's identity. He was twenty-one-year-old Carl Forbes—a first cousin of the victim who'd died in the shooting.

"Carl, are you really a racist or a wannabe?" the officer asked from the front seat of his cruiser. He had already spoken to several witnesses who had unbelievably approached him and volunteered their eyewitness testimony as soon as he arrived on scene, so he was already leery of the man he had in his custody.

"I'm whatever you want me to be, officer," the man responded. "Are you really a cop or a wannabe?"

"I wasn't being sarcastic, Carl," the officer told him. "Most people that have strong racist views don't usually walk around wearing billboards on their t-shirts, and, for the record, I've never known a criminal to stay on the scene after committing a crime. I could be wrong, but nothing about you rings authentic to me."

"I guess you have a right to your opinion," the man said before lowering his head to his chest. "When will the officer be charged for killing my cousin?"

The officer paused before answering. He heard nothing but pain in the young man's voice. "Probably never because he didn't do anything wrong."

"Bullshit, he ruined my family!" he said while sitting erectly, a large vein appearing on the side of his neck.

"Your cousin was the one committing a felony, Carl," the officer explained. "The choice he made is what cost him his life. No one made him go out and rob that store."

"Robbing a store didn't give someone the right to kill him, did it?" the man said as his voice cracked.

"I understand your frustration, sir. Believe me I do," the officer said. "It didn't give anyone the right to kill him, you're right about that, but the investigation is still ongoing...let's wait and see what happens once it's complete." The officer kept his car in park—he had no intentions of taking the man to jail.

Carl's shoulders slumped forward as he relaxed. His breathing became normal, appreciating the officer for treating him with respect. A respect he felt should be reciprocated. "Thanks for being understanding and sympathetic," he said with a sigh.

"You seem like a really nice guy, Carl. Tell me about your shirt."

"Ahhh, it's just some bullshit crap someone gave me to put on...said I'd be the first suspect when the cops hit the scene."

"You didn't start these fires did you, Carl?"

"No, I had nothing to do with it," he said before sighing.

"I know you didn't," the officer told him. "Witnesses told us you just stood by and watched...told us you were coerced into being the fall guy."

Carl Forbes became silent. He wasn't a criminal, and had never been in trouble with the law before, not even something as diminutive as a traffic ticket. Tears welled in his eyes as he looked at the officer. "They're right, I didn't do this," he said as tears and snot rolled down his face.

"Do you know the names of those that did?"

"I don't know their names," Carl told him.

"I believe you, so I won't press you to snitch," the officer said calmly. "I think you and your family has been through enough, Carl. You've already lost your cousin, so it'll make no sense in me taking you to jail, especially for a crime I know you didn't do."

"Thank you, sir…you're proof that not all officers are bad people. If Shane would have gotten you he'd still be alive."

"Thanks for the compliment, Carl," the policeman said. "Let the process run its course before you pass judgment, okay? You may learn that there are other good officers out there as well. Let me remove those cuffs and send you on your way."

"That'll be great," said Carl.

"I'm gonna grab a shirt from my trunk too. A good guy like you shouldn't be wearing that one…and don't ever again try to take the fall for something you didn't do, okay?"

"Alright," he said with a nod.

The officer gave him a shirt from his trunk and let him go. The fires were out before he left the scene. Piles of debris doused with gasoline inside of large steel trash bins were the only things that burned—the stadium itself was never threatened.

CHAPTER 10

Miss Fontenot, an adorable, medium-sized woman from the deep south, who did a great job of keeping herself up, and also an English teacher at Alexander Shaw High School, was a sweetheart in every sense of the word. She was a spiritual woman, very strong in her faith, who tried hard not to let her faith interfere with her job, but she refused to ignore anything God placed on her heart.

She knew for a fact that enough pressure could form diamonds, but she was also of the opinion that it could turn people into gems.

She stood inside the doorway of her classroom, watching students as they went to their lockers after their lunch break, when she witnessed a commotion between two of her students.

"Rodney, can you please leave me alone?" Ke'Auna said, clearly agitated.

"Why are you acting so stuck up?" said Rodney as he stood by her locker.

"I'm not acting stuck up. I just don't have time for no damn boys."

"I'm just asking to eat lunch with you tomorrow, Ke'Auna. It's not like I'm tryin' to get in your pants or nothin.' Damn!"

"I don't want to eat lunch with you, Rodney. Not today, tomorrow or any other time."

Rodney had had enough and was getting ready to walk away until he realized they had an audience, that's when he felt an incredible need to show out. "I didn't wanna eat lunch with your stuck up ass anyway—once-a-month-bleedin' bitch! You ain't gon' give nobody no play, so you might as well go get that pussy infibulated."

"*Oooh,*" said one of the spectators, knowing he had said something bad, but was unsure what it was.

"Rodney, leave her alone!" Heather said, stepping forward from the crowd, after trying her hardest not to get involved. "Why can't you just respect what my friend is saying? No, you wanna get all hostile and disrespectful. How would you like it if someone said that to your mom?"

Ke'Auna was surprised to see Heather come to her defense. They hadn't said anything to each other in several days, so it wasn't what she had expected to hear. "Thank you," she said as she hugged her, feeling her young precious heart as it deflated from sighing.

"You're welcome," said Heather. "I miss you."

"I miss you, too."

44

Rodney smiled when the two girls hugged—he was actually relieved to see them talking to each other. "I'm sorry, Ke'Auna. You know I didn't mean it."

"Then why'd you say it?" Heather blurted out.

"That last part wasn't part of the plan. I honestly don't know where that came from. But Miss Fontenot is the one who put me up to it."

"Miss Fontenot?" Ke'Auna said. "But, why?"

"It worked, so apparently she knew somethin' we didn't," said Rodney. "Are we cool— do you accept my apology?"

"Yeah, we're cool, Rodney," Ke'Auna smiled.

"What about y'all—are y'all cool?"

"Of course we are," said Heather as she pressed her cheek against Ke'Auna's shoulder, and draped her arm over the back of her neck.

They all looked toward Miss Fontenot's classroom. She stood smiling in her doorway with her arms crossed, then uncrossed them and gave them a thumbs up. She went back inside her classroom when they returned the gesture.

"Do you wanna come over and play nurse this evening?" asked Heather.

"I'd love to," said Ke'Auna. "Thanks again, and I'll see you after school."

Not wanting to be late for class, Heather backed away and said, "Later."

Matthew Sinclair, in full paramedic uniform, creased down to the bone, parked the ambulance in front of his residence and hopped out quickly to go look for his daughter. It was against hospital policy for any first-responder to take emergency vehicles to their home, but he'd promised Heather countless times that he'd figure out a way to make it happen. It made him feel good to finally be able to surprise her.

She had been so adamant to him about someday becoming a registered nurse, so he wanted to inspire her to hold onto her dream.

He entered his home and yelled out her name, regretting not giving her a call to give her a heads up, but he had no idea the opportunity would present itself without issuing a warning.

He was relieved when he saw her galloping down the hallway with her friend in tow. He knew the two girls hadn't been talking, so he was glad to see them together again. He decided not to mention it because it held no relevance—he decided to carry on as if things were normal.

"Hey, dad. What's up?" she said with a huge smile on her face, then wrapped her arms around his waist and gave him a hug.

"I got a surprise for you and Ke'Auna outside," he said as he looked back and forth between the two girls.

"Oooh, dad. Are you serious? No way."

"Sure. I told you I'd do it, but we gotta make it quick so I can return it, okay?"

"Okay," said Heather, smiling uncontrollably.

"What is it?" asked Ke'Auna.

46

"Come on," said Heather as she headed toward the front door to go outside. She had never even mentioned it to Ke'Auna before, because she didn't think her dad would ever pull it off. He'd made so many excuses in the past about why he couldn't do it, so she'd stopped looking forward to it, thinking it would never happen.

Matt surveyed the street when they got outside, making sure no one was watching that could get him in trouble. He hurried down the driveway to his service vehicle and pulled open the driver's side door and let the girls hop in.

"This is so cool," Ke'Auna said, looking around at all the switches and buttons. It reminded her of the scenes she'd seen on TV whenever they showed someone being transported to the hospital after sustaining an injury.

Heather reiterated, "This is cool, dad. Do you know how all this stuff works?"

"I sure do," her dad said proudly. He climbed in after them and pulled the door shut. He pointed out the siren, explaining that the vehicle was really a mobile hospital, equipped with everything that was needed to keep a patient alive until he could get them transported to one of the area hospitals.

Instead of risking being seen by showing them the back of the ambulance, Matt pointed out different things, using his finger, and gave a brief description.

The girls were in awe as they learned about the makeshift hospital on wheels whose only purpose was to preserve life. It made them want more than ever to become RN's.

Matthew looked around more before opening the door and stepping out of the vehicle. He helped Heather then Ke'Auna as they climbed out, then hugged them both simultaneously as they thanked him repeatedly. He climbed back inside the vehicle and sped off, leaving both girls happy and filled with hope. He was delighted to see them be friends again. They went back inside the house and locked the door.

CHAPTER 11

The high-ranked officer sat reclined in his chair, contemplating with his eyes shut, fingers clasped on the back of his head, feet resting on papers atop his desk—on the clock getting paid to do absolutely nothing. The jury was still out as to whether or not his lack of honestly earning his income was the American way, or just the way of Police Chief Scott Dunlap, who'd already been fired once from a job for being lazy. It seemed the higher the rank, the bigger the salary—the less work he wanted to do—a mindset that seemed to run rampant in those who worked in government.

I'm not getting paid enough for this shit he said to himself, unwrapping his feet and placing them delicately on the floor beneath his desk. He was still loathing over a call he'd received from Mayor Kason two days before, of which he felt his job had been threatened.

It had been ten days since the fatal shooting of the nineteen-year-old, and the public was still demanding that the officer be charged—they promised the protests would continue until charges are brought.

The mayor was spooked. It was him who'd warned the chief that heads would roll if they didn't find a way to appease the public.

Chief Dunlap downed the rest of his Frappuccino. He adjusted his Bluetooth to fit more comfortably in his ear before placing his finger on the touch-screen of his phone to answer a call. "What's up, lieutenant?"

"Hello, chief, it's been a while since anyone has addressed me in that manner. I'm calling to see where we're at with the investigation?"

"Well, I don't know, Kevin. I haven't heard anything," the chief lied. "I'm playing it by ear just like you."

It wasn't exactly what he'd hoped to hear, but all he could do was roll with the punches. "It's been a week and a half and I'm ready to come back to work. I'm getting pretty restless sitting around the house."

"I know what you mean," the chief told him. "Well, you can't beat yourself up about it; you can always look at it as a vacation, Kevin."

"I'm not in the mood for any jokes, chief. You can save the humor for someone else."

"Have you heard anything from Internal Affairs?"

"Nothing."

"I guess no news is good news for now," the chief told him.

"Is there anything you can do to speed up the process?"

"Not without compromising the department—I think it's best to let things naturally run its course."

"I understand that, chief," replied the lieutenant. "I'm just thinking that maybe you could make a phone call, send a text, email, fax, tweet or something to somebody to at least get me cleared to come back to work? I got protesters walking up and down the street where I live. I can't stand this shit being around my family."

"Sorry to hear that, Kevin," the chief told him. "Something should happen soon. Let's see what happens in the next day or two."

"Alright," said the lieutenant. "Talk to you soon."

"Don't call me I'll call you," the chief told him, then nodded his head and sighed when he hung up.

Summer Sinclair shut down the lights, set the alarm and locked the door to her office. She was somewhat weary but in high spirits, and looked forward to going home and snuggling up to her husband, after a long hot bath and a hot meal. She reached down and removed her heels, one at a time, from her aching feet, and carried them in her hand as she strode leisurely down the red-brick pathway in front of her office, just as she'd done several times before to get to her vehicle, which was parked directly at the end of the manmade walkway, about forty or fifty feet in front of her business.

It was barely after 5PM but already dark. She wished there were a couple more streetlights in the area to brighten things up a bit, but her office porch light would have to suffice.

She tossed her purse and shoes onto the passenger seat before climbing behind the wheel and pulling the door shut. She was glad the workweek was over with and welcomed a couple of days off, just thinking about it made her body relax. She allowed herself to sink into her car's soft-leather interior. She figured a few minutes of quality relaxation could do her body some good before beginning her trip to her humble abode, but her phone rang as soon as her upper and lower eyelids came together, she looked at the caller ID before answering. "Hi Dan, or would you rather I call you Judge Silva?" she said with a giggle.

"Either is fine with me," he said in a calm soothing voice. "I hope this isn't a bad time but I was hoping I could see you?"

"Your timing couldn't be worse, Dan. I'm sorry," she said. "Where are you?"

"At the Vdara Hotel. I checked in about an hour ago."

"I had a late day, Dan. I'm actually sitting inside my car still parked in front of my office. My day just ended, literally minutes ago. I just want to go home, eat and take a shower. Maybe we can get together sometime tomorrow?"

Judge Silva shut his eyes and let everything she'd said sink in a bit. He had instant regrets about renting a room without first consulting her about his strong ambitions to meet with her— hearing her response made him believe he'd gone out on a limb for nothing, the only thing he could think of was making love to her, he had no desire to be with anyone else. "That's too bad, Summer. I was really hoping we could hangout tonight. You're only ten, maybe fifteen minutes away, are you sure you don't wanna swing by for a while? I'll really make it worth your while, I promise," he said, feeling cavalier.

In the past, men had shown her time and time again that they would do almost anything to sample her goods, so she wasn't the least bit surprised to hear him beg. It wasn't the typical *please, pretty please* style of begging that's known to most people, but for a head honcho such as Judge Silva, who was accustomed to giving orders instead of pleading for mercy, his level of politeness could easily be construed as begging.

"Your request is so tempting, Dan, but I'm tired and need to get home to my family," she said, seductively.

"Ohh, you sound so sexy, Summer," he said, fighting his inner demons. "I just took a steamy-hot shower, now I'm lying here naked with an aching, throbbing, attention-seeking erection, wishing you could put your mouth on it or hide it inside you, now I'm wondering if I should feel rejected since you don't wanna come see me?"

"I'm not rejecting you, Dan. You know I wouldn't do that," she said softly. "I really wish I could be there with you, Dan. I really do."

He heard something in her voice that made him believe her. He recalled their last encounter in the Tuscany Suites, when she'd worn a tiny pair of pink booty-shorts, of which her rounded ass cheeks peeked tendentiously beneath, if only she could be in his presence now, he thought.

She thought of how uncomfortable he must feel lying in bed by himself with a hard-on. Her thoughts then drifted to Kerry and the fact that they hadn't spoken in nearly a week, but that was something she would have to worry about later—she had to return her focus to the business at hand. "Dan, if I were in that bed with you right now, I wouldn't want you to make love to me, I'd need you to fuck me!"

"Oh, Summer, I'd love to," he said as he visualized her bending over in front of him, exposing her delicious-looking strawberry delight from the back, his hand began caressing his erect phallus.

"I wish I could suck your balls and move them all around inside my hot mouth, then take your hard dick down my throat, slowly, deeply, over and over again, sucking and licking it up and down, just the way you like it, Dan," she said in a breathy-aggressive-like voice. "Your dick should be inside your hand by now."

"Oh, believe me, it is," he said before issuing a light groan. His own hand was not what he'd hoped to get, but it was better than nothing, and since he was mentally, emotionally, and verbally with the woman he wanted to be with, he was certain it beat being alone by a long-shot.

Summer became more turned on as she listened to the masculinity in his voice. She found her legs sprawled in the drivers seat of her car, skirt rose high on her thigh, her right foot rested atop the passenger seat with her hand stuffed inside her panties, rubbing hardly on her clit. Her head crouched snugly below the window between the seat and door. She knew how much he enjoyed performing cunnilingus on her, and as sweaty and sticky as she was, she wished his tongue was on her clit instead of her finger. She thought it would be a good idea to bring it to his attention.

"Dan, my pussy is so hot and wet. I wish you could taste it."

Judge Silva visualized her wet pink vagina, and knew how sweet it tasted from the multiple times he'd buried his face in it and allowed her to straddle his face in the past, he thrust his hips forward harder to match the rhythm of his hand. "My god, Summer. I'd love to put my mouth on your pussy. I'd love nothing more right now than to eat your pussy and asshole, and I wouldn't stop until you begged me to."

"Ooooh, Dan. I want you to come in my mouth. Come in my mouth and make me swallow your cum!" she said as she slipped into ecstasy, visualizing herself aggressively sucking his dick with his hand behind her head, forcing her. She could see his tongue lapping away at her clit, up and down between her labia, then in-between her butt cheeks to lick her asshole. She felt herself get weaker as her juices poured from her, orgasm flowing in bursts all over and in-between her fingers. She couldn't believe what had just happened.

She heard him moaning at the same time as she relieved herself and knew that he had reached his apex as well. She had a female client in jail for prostitution who was scheduled to go before him the following week. She hoped it was plausible to use the phone call as leverage to get her set free, or to possibly be able to offer her clients' sexual services? She rid herself of the thought. She'd cross that line when she got to it.

"Have a good night, Summer and, thank you," he said, tired.

"You too, Dan. I might call you tomorrow."

"I'll be somewhere," he said then hung up.

Summer smiled to herself as she looked in the mirror on the visor above her. She quickly pulled herself together after spraying air-freshener inside her car and letting down the windows.

She texted Matt and told him she was on her way home. She began having second thoughts about snuggling with him. She figured she'd probably just call it a night after soaking in a hot bath and eating something. She would have a nightcap and play the rest by ear.

CHAPTER 12

It took nearly two weeks, but the day finally came when the shit hit the fan. Protests and demonstrations—some peaceful/some violent—took place all over the city, it was plastered on every station airing the local news— the metropolis Las Vegas looked more like the city of Beirut. Countless fires, assaults, batteries, and other forms of vandalism and mayhem were happening repeatedly, night after night, for eleven straight days, after consistent chaos something finally broke, and when it did, the destruction ceased almost immediately.

Twelve days after the deadly shooting of unarmed teenager Shane Forbes, Lieutenant Kevin Gaines was formally charged with second-degree murder and taken into custody without incident. There were a lot of mixed feelings about his arrest.

He sat heartbroken inside an interrogation room at the Clark County jail, in a section of the jail that was usually reserved for disgraced officers and police informants. "Chief, I don't understand. Why is this happening?" he said, confused.

"I'm sorry, Kevin. I had no other choice."

"I didn't violate any laws," explained the shamed lieutenant. "Why are you doing this, you know this is wrong?"

The chief hesitated before speaking. He had a hard time looking at the lieutenant of whom he highly respected, but he knew there were no other options—he had to do what he had to do. "You left me no other choice, Kevin. If you'd just taken the few seconds it would have took to activate your body or dash cam, none of this would be happening," he said. "Now you'll have to deal with it in the court of law. I'm sorry."

"So many unarmed black men and women have been killed at the hands of white officers, and not one white officer was at fault? All were justified, even in cases where it was clearly murder," he said before pausing. "I don't get it, as soon as a white boy dies, I'm charged with murder for protecting my life. I guess my black life doesn't matter, huh?"

"C'mon, Kevin, don't make this an issue about race," the chief told him. "This has nothing to do with race, believe me."

"So why the fuck am I in jail when you know as well as me that I've done nothing wrong?"

"I'm sure the public's outcry has something to do with it," the chief admitted. "The protests, the violence, the call for justice and resignations—it's too out of control and we need it to stop."

"The same thing happened in all of the other cases when white officers killed blacks and it didn't matter. Why does it matter now when the dynamics are reversed?"

"Similar things have occurred in the past, yes, but nothing of this magnitude, not even close," the chief said. "Arresting you wasn't my call, Kevin."

"What…whose was it?"

"Only one person is over me, you know that."

Lieutenant Gaines looked at the chief, and after an awkward silence he uttered, "Mayor Kason."

"That's between me and you. I guess the pressure must've got to him."

"So where's my support? What happened to the blue wall, the code of silence, the brotherhood that all of the white officers got when they killed unarmed black people? No one from the department is speaking up for me. Not even you, chief."

"I tried but it didn't work. I'm sorry."

"Apparently you didn't try hard enough. I'm sorry too."

"I have to go, Kevin. Call me if there's anything I can do to help. I'm rooting for you."

Kevin Gaines watched the chief leave. He'd been admiring the man for twenty-five years and, in only a few minutes, he lost all the respect he had for him. It became transparent exactly what kind of people he worked for—something he would have never believed if he hadn't experienced it himself.

He knew his career in law enforcement was probably over, especially since the decision had been reached to arrest him. He began to understand that no matter how hard he worked, how high he ranked, how much integrity he had or how much he tried to exemplify what it meant to be a positive male role-model for all of the fatherless black youth in the city of Las Vegas, he would never be equal to his white counterparts, especially in the eyes of the law.

The law viewed him as a criminal even though he wasn't one, and it could have only been because of his skin color, he thought. He lowered his face in his hands and began to sob. The revelation was too much to bear—it revealed an image that he had been blind to.

To his knowledge, America had always been a country that had problems when it came to race-relations, but he thought his city was different since its makeup consisted of so many different cultures, but he now knew that his beloved city was part of the problem.

It appeared to him that the eyes of the law were the eyes of whites. Black people had no chance when it came to justice, not even within the police department. His thoughts were: when it came to injustice it was *'just-us.'*

In hindsight his brain began to formulate the systematic pattern. He was being charged with second-degree murder and would face trial because the victim in his case happened to be a person of a lighter skin. In the cases where white officers had killed unarmed black people, whether justified or unjustified, it was the black victim that was put on trial, not the officer. It was a picture that became more and more disturbing as he thought about it. It seemed the system was designed for the blacks to always lose and for the whites to always win, no matter the side.

Tears rolled down his face and between his fingers like levees had broken. He thought of his wife and his young daughter—how in the world would he be able to escape the trap, he wondered? The only thing he could do was leave it up to God.

CHAPTER 13

Retired prostitute Amy Forbes kept quiet even after she learned of the arrest of the officer she believed selfishly shot her son. The local news was her only source of information, so she watched it religiously to stay up-to-date.

She had her son cremated the same week he was killed. She hoped to be able to put the painful chapter of her life behind her, but it seemed every time she turned on the news, they were discussing the protests, marches, demonstrations, fires and violence of all sorts—mobs of strangers called for justice in Shane's honor—demanding the mayor and chief to step down from their posts, or bring charges against the officer who'd murdered her son.

It saddened her that her only son had been forever silenced, but it made her proud to see so many groups of strangers take to the streets to stand together in solidarity to become his voice. She was grateful their voices didn't go unheard, and that their calls for justice was not in vain.

Shane Forbes came from a broken home. His dad Clay was in prison serving a harsh sentence of life without the possibility of parole for murdering a security guard during a jewelry store robbery. His only sibling Laura, four years his senior, was strung out on prescription pills and methamphetamine, often went missing, sometimes for months at a time as though she'd fallen off the face of the earth, but, in her right mind, and within reason, there wasn't anything she wouldn't do for her younger brother.

There were a few cousins, aunts, uncles and nephews who were Forbes', but Shane, who also struggled with substance abuse to help him cope, was not exceptionally close to anyone, not even his mom.

She was genuinely surprised to see so many people cared and wanted justice for him, and she hoped he was smiling down on them from Heaven?

She looked over at the urn that held his ashes and wished she had been a better mom, but knew it was much too late to fret.

Amy was comforted by the thought that her son was in a better place. She knew that no matter what happened to the officer that had taken his life, Shane would never be brought back— her plan was to remain in the shadows and watch it all unfold.

CHAPTER 14

A soft pleasure-filled moan escaped her throat. She placed her small delicate hands firmly on his pecks to balance herself as she ground her pelvis gracefully onto his shaft. Back and forth. Up and down. Round and round. Riding him deeply. Swiftly. Forcefully. Turning the slippery canal of her vagina into a suctioning cup as she squeezed her muscles to pleasure him.

She continued to moan as she gyrated her hips, swerving her body like a seasoned belly-dancer while arching her back, moaning louder and louder as her orgasm neared—she knew she wouldn't be able to hold back much longer. "Oh my god. Ohh god!" she screamed when he squeezed her breasts and nipples simultaneously, bringing her closer and closer to her ultimate release.

"You never cease to amaze me, Mrs. Sinclair."

"You're amazing too, Kevin. You never cease to please me," she said before stiffening. "Oh my god—oooh, I'm coming. Ahhh, ahhh, ooohh yesss.

Mmmm," she said while biting her bottom lip, which was quivering uncontrollably when it escaped her teeth. "You should probably go home to your wife now. I'm sure the last couple days have been rough for her."

Summer had picked him up from jail less than an hour earlier when he was released on his own recognizance—she knew his decision to call her could only mean one thing.

The two had been hooking up secretly for nearly three years, and because she was a woman who appreciated endowment, Kevin Gaines was the only man who truly fulfilled her. She loved the way he felt inside of her, the way he stretched her out and filled her to capacity, and although it filled her with guilt every time she saw or spoke to Kerry, she knew in her heart of hearts that she would never stop spreading her legs for him. To her, his sex was magnificent, absolutely amazing, something she swore she needed in her life, everything he did to her body drove her absolutely nuts. She didn't take anything away from her husband Matt, he was okay, but he wasn't Kevin. Size and skillwise, there was no comparison.

"Yeah, you're right," he said as he placed his hands on her slim waist and helped her climb off of him, she then reached into her center console and handed him a couple of baby wipes so they could clean themselves up. "That was great as always," he said, kind of thinking out loud.

"You got that right," she said while gathering her clothes.

"You will be representing me when I go to court, right?"

It wasn't exactly the kind of conversation she was expecting to have after their roll in the hay, but she detected in his voice what she thought was nervousness. "The Police Union will appoint you one of its lawyers. Let's first see how that goes. If they try to screw you, then I'll take over."

"Alright, you know I'm going to hold you to it," he said while arching his brows. "You best get me home, I'm sure my wife is missing me. Drop me off in the usual spot."

The beautiful defense attorney did as instructed. She rushed to drop off her best friend's husband around the corner from his home and let him walk the rest of the way.

Kerry ran straight into his arms as soon as he entered the house, guilt swept over him as soon as he saw her.

"Hello, handsome, I miss you."

"I miss you too, baby," he said as he leaned down to kiss her, pulling her closely into his arms then cuffed her buttocks.

"How'd you get home?"

"Walked."

"From downtown? Why didn't you call me, you know I would have picked you up. C'mon baby?"

"I know, baby. I wanted to ease my mind and walk some tension off," he lied. "I need to get in the shower, I feel disgusting."

"You smell it too," she said, frowning and scrunching her top lip. "Go ahead and wash that jail-smell off you. I'll fix you something to eat, I'm sure you're hungry, right?"

"I am," he said as he smacked her on the backside and headed toward the bedroom. He was relieved that her inquisitions weren't more extensive, for a second, he didn't know where her questioning was headed.

Ke'Auna exited her bedroom after hearing his voice, "Hi, daddy. Glad you're home."

"Hey baby, daddy missed you so much."

"I missed you too," she said as she embraced him. "Why did you have to go to jail, I thought you were the one who put people in jail?"

"It's a long story, baby. We're not always treated as fairly as others. One day I'm going to sit down and tell you all about it."

"I already know, daddy," she said smiling. "I experience it all the time when I'm with Heather. People treat me differently than they do her."

For some reason he wasn't surprised, but the last person he wanted to discuss racism with was his fourteen-year-old. "Sorry to hear that sweetheart. Hopefully things will someday get better for us."

"They will, daddy," she said with confidence as if she knew something he didn't.

"Daddy needs to go ahead and take a shower, your mom just finished telling me how much I stink. Go tell her to put a steak on the grill for me."

Ke'Auna smiled as she dismissed herself, heading to the kitchen to accompany her mom.

Kevin disappeared inside his bedroom to go bathe himself, wondering how his ordeal would play out in court?

CHAPTER 15

The car rounded the corner and was brought to a complete stop before the headlights extinguished under the light fog. It wasn't a vehicle that was familiar to anyone who resided on Beech Family Street, or any of its surrounding streets, so it piqued the interest of a neighbor as soon as it rested in front of the Gaines' residence.

It was the time of morning when cat burglars, streetwalkers, night stalkers and other criminals who operated under the shadow of darkness, ended their shifts, commonly referred to as vampire hours. Cars were usually backing out of driveways and pulling away from curbs at this time of morning, as residents left for work—any cars coming instead of going were guaranteed to pique someone's interest, especially in a neighborhood such as Oceanblue Estates.

Kerry had just finished some early morning pruning and was up from her knees after tending to her garden when she noticed the wine-colored car, which looked to her to be a Lexus or a Toyota Camry, if she couldn't see the logo, she had a difficult time differentiating between the two models.

She stood motionless, holding a metal pale full of gardening tools as she stared at the car, which continued to sit oddly in the center of the street. The dark-colored tint on its windows made it impossible to see who was driving or how many times the car was occupied, but it made her nervous, and she wondered if it was time for her family to consider moving? More and more unwanted guests had been flocking to the area over the past couple of weeks, ever since the shooting of Shane Forbes, most of the neighbors had been group-texting daily to keep each other abreast—they took great pride in their neighborhood watch program, they weren't aware of any other neighborhood that took it more seriously.

Strangers were seen walking up and down the sidewalks at all times of the night—there had been reports of some obscenities yelled and other mild disturbances and unruly behavior, but thus far, there was no sign of violence, and Kerry found herself hoping that it wasn't about to change.

Her husband had just returned home from jail the evening before, and after having received countless unwanted phone calls and death threats, she wasn't sure if the car's occupant or occupants were there to harm her husband; the thought alone made the hair stand up on the back of her neck. She knew that whomever was driving the car was watching her as she watched them. Her attention was averted when a neighbor across the street backed out of his driveway and pulled up behind the vehicle as it sat stationary in the center of the road—it shot forward as if it had been rammed or projected from a cannon—whoever was inside would remain a mystery, at least for now.

Now that the immediate threat was gone, Kerry's mental faculties returned back to proper working order. She wished she had ran out into the street and tried to capture the car's license plate number, or the driver's identity, but after giving it some thought, she knew it would have been a waste of time.

She stood five feet five and weighed one hundred and seventy pounds, her ass, breasts, thighs and hips accounted for half of it, nonetheless, she had no immediate plans to change any of it. There was no need to. She regularly received compliments from men and women on how thick and fine she was—compliments she was more than certain she'd never get tired of hearing.

She went back inside the house and took a hot shower. Thoughts lingered in the back of her mind about the suspicious vehicle she'd encountered just moments earlier. She finished showering and prepared a hearty breakfast for her husband; scrambled eggs; bacon; buttered toast; cheese grits; orange juice—the works. She was indecisive as to whether or not she should share the morning's activities with him? She really didn't want to, to not cause any problems or unnecessary worry, but she knew it was in the best interest of the family to let him know. She knew she would also have to inform Ke'Auna—the safety of her family was priority.

CHAPTER 16

For the past six months, the weekends were the most active and the most challenging for the Las Vegas Metropolitan Police Department, especially when it came to violent crimes, such as robbery, domestic violence, sexual assault and murder in the city of Las Vegas. Calls usually began coming in Friday evening between seven and eight after a large number of people received their paychecks and began drinking, simultaneously celebrating as they put a long hard workweek behind them, looking forward to a couple of days off. Not all celebrations would remain peaceful, that's when the Las Vegas Metropolitan Police Department sprung into action—Fire and Rescue were sometimes called as well, but that was for the weekends that were considered normal.

This particular weekend in the metropolis was anything but normal, especially inside the headquarters of the police department.

Chief Dunlap was normally the superior officer. Every officer and rank was well beneath him, anything that happened or didn't happen was either approved or denied by him alone, but on this particular day, every officer was quiet, including him, because a bigger kahuna than him was in the building, and every officer, regardless of rank, had to bow down to him.

Mayor Kason was the city's top dog and had been for a year and a half, but had never been inside metro's headquarters before, so for him to be there, everyone knew something big was on the horizon.

Officers were sneaking peeks through the partially closed blinds as they strode past Chief Dunlap's office, for no other reason than to be nosy.

Mayor Kason stood pointing his finger as he spoke calmly to the chief—there was no need to be aggressive; everyone knew full well that he was in charge.

"Sir, I don't understand what you mean when you say I'll have to put my personal feelings aside. My feelings have nothing to do with what's happening to Lieutenant Gaines."

"Ex-Lieutenant," said Mayor Kason. "I've gotten all the backlash I can handle for one case. What happened had to be done. If he hadn't been arrested and charged, my chances of re-election would be zero, so would your chances of continuing to be the Chief of Police."

Chief Dunlap's throat was too dry to reply. He walked over to the water cooler and poured himself a glass and pondered what the mayor uttered as he took a sip. "So, is this case more about politics than anything else? Are you worried about facing a smear-campaign when you run for your second term?"

"I can't say the thought never crossed my mind, but it's not the only thing that matters," said Mayor Kason, turning a shade redder as if he couldn't believe one of his underlings was questioning his authority.

Chief Dunlap noticed the change in his superior's demeanor and knew it wouldn't be wise of him to keep treading down that path. He felt smaller than he had in a long time, the experience alone, was humbling. "Kevin was an excellent lieutenant," he said in a voice that was barely louder than a whisper. " He's a good man. I hate to see this happening to him."

"Don't be so hard on yourself, chief. It's not your fault what goes on behind closed doors. Due process did what it was supposed to do. The fact-finding review board is to blame here, not us. They're the ones who decided he should be terminated and charged. All we did was give our opinions," the mayor said nonchalantly, as if his opinion was harmless.

"It's the 'closed doors' part that worries me," said Chief Dunlap. "That's where money secretly exchanges hands, weapons, threats and tactics are used and deployed and go unexposed, documents are shredded and burned and never recovered, and new documents are fabricated and executed as originals. Those are the same closed doors you're talking about, right? If those doors or walls could talk, they'd probably be yelling *don't witness this shit!*"

"I've never been moved by speculation, chief. Facts are the only things that move me."

"I'll keep that in mind, mayor. Is this meeting adjourned?"

"I believe it is," he said as he adjusted his tie, his personal way of flexing his power.

Mayor Kason left police headquarters with his head held high, although he felt in his heart that he'd been too lenient. His next stop was the Clark County Commission Building. He had other matters to tend to.

CHAPTER 17

The two bodies glistened with sweat as the forbidden sex continued for nearly two-and-a-half hours. Summer Sinclair was all about business. Her mouth salivated as she stared straight into the eye of the erect penis as she leaned toward it, the owner of the penis far from her mind.

She thrust her hips downward; grinding as she pressed her swollen clitoris hard against his tongue, then sunk her mouth lower, deeply onto the phallus that stood erectly before her—she relaxed her throat muscles and received it in its entirety. Oral sex was her preference. To her, it was less invasive than having someone plowing repeatedly into her—she also thought it was easier and more convenient. For her, giving head was like walking or drinking water—it took little to no effort, and was normal to her. If she didn't suck dick, it was abnormal.

She felt at ease as she continued to do something she knew she was good at, but her body was still trembling and had a noticeable ache, more than likely from the percussion that happened earlier when he rammed his rod in and out of her asshole, one of the very reasons she preferred oral.

She sucked harder on his rod, deeper, then faster while cupping his balls with her hand— it wasn't long before she felt his load deep in her throat. "Mmmm, yummy," she said as she licked the head of his penis, directly on the hole the jism had spewed. "I want it all; give it to me."

"Great blowjob, Summer," said Governor Pitts as he pulled her up close to lay beside him. "Excellent job!"

"Does that performance put me ahead in favors?" she asked before kissing his chest and massaging his soft phallus with her wandering hand.

"Your blowjobs are always great, Summer. It's not like you did something different this time."

"You bounced up and down in this ass too, let's not forget that," she said, reminding him. "You can't say you get to do that often."

I do it every day, just not with you he said to himself. He hadn't realized his lawyer friend was so naïve. She was just one of his many sluts that he had on call, apparently, she thought she was the only one? *Oh well* he thought.

"Hello. Are you in there; did you hear what I said?"

"Oh, sorry," said Governor Pitts. "You're right. Can't say I do that every day. Yeah, I guess it does give you a little leeway. I'd say at least two."

"That'll be great. Thank you," said Summer. "Two or three back-to-back would put me back on track to getting my popularity back. It's been dry for me a long time," she said in a dreamy-like state.

"We'll fix it for you, don't worry about it," the governor told her. He was in town for a day to attend a meeting about funding a new freeway project. Summer was always on his list of things-to-do whenever he was in town for any reason. It's how she got nearly all of her clients clemency at the Nevada Board of Pardons, her goal was to get two favors at a time, but she hadn't had any luck for the past few years. Governor Pitts told her it was for political reasons. According to him, politics in Nevada came before anything else, no matter how many families it left in shambles.

Now that he was once again ready to start granting clemencies, she already knew which two of her clients she wanted out first.

They showered and got dressed before going downstairs to the bar where they had a cocktail. Her anus throbbed, sending shockwaves of pleasure through her body as she sat on the stool at the end of the bar, discussing some of Governor Pitts future plans about solar energy in both Reno and Vegas. It wasn't a topic she was knowledgeable or interested in, but he wanted to share it with her, so she listened intently, or at least pretended to.

The governor revealed that he wouldn't be in Vegas again for at least another eight or nine months, unless something unforeseen called for his presence. She would be in touch with him no matter how long it took, and whenever he returned, she'd be ready for him.

Several high-ranked officials, in and out of town, relied on her. Whenever any of them needed her, she was at their beck and call.

Summer parted ways with Governor Pitts and went to the gym. Her body was in need of a thorough workout.

CHAPTER 18

It had been months since the two buddies set aside an evening to hang out together, their lives, with no planning, had headed in two separate directions. The TapDatAzz Gentlemen's Club in rural Las Vegas was one of their favorite places to frequent and chat it up as friends, the atmosphere was always relaxed and professional—there was always a wide variety of eye candy to peruse and be entertained by—all of the women were tasty-looking and carried themselves with class. The night was shaping up to be a beautiful one.

"Gentlemen, would you like a refill on your drinks?" asked a cocktail waitress when she pranced up and stopped in front of their table, standing only four feet eleven, but incredibly curvaceous. "Kevin, I know you want another beer, right?" she said flirtatiously.

"Yes, Jacqueline, please," he said smiling. "You already knew the answer, so why did you waste your breath asking such a dumb question, you could have saved that breath for something more productive," he joked.

"Like what?" she said with her brows raised, smiling from ear to ear, hand on her hip, awaiting his answer.

He looked at Matt for help, then back at her, before shrugging his shoulders and saying, "I don't know."

They all burst out laughing. Kevin had once again put his foot in his mouth, something he'd been known to do in the past from time to time.

"What about you, Matt, would you like another Hennessey?"

"Yes, please. I'm drinking as long as he is, we don't believe in letting each other drink alone."

Jacqueline looked back and forth between Matt and Kevin, then looked directly at Matt and spoke candidly, "Don't forget one of you has to drive the other home. That means one of you has to be responsible enough to know when enough is enough. There are already too many crazies on the road. It would be unwise to add to it. Be smart and make this the last round," she said before walking off.

Kevin and Matt frowned as they looked at each other because they both knew they'd already over consumed.

"You know she's right, right?" said Matt.

"Women always are," replied Kevin.

"Why'd she bother asking if that's how she felt?"

Kevin shrugged his shoulders while downing the rest of his beer.

"She went from flirting with you, to a mother figure. I don't get it," Matt said, confused.

"I do. She cares, man," Kevin said. "That's how she is. You know if I hadn't met Kerry, Jacqueline and I probably would have gotten married. She's a sweet woman. Small in stature but makes up for it in heart."

"I know she's adorable, Kev, but you better never let Kerry hear you say that," Matt said with a slur.

"I didn't hear nothin', did someone say somethin'? Kevin said, smiling. "No, man, Jacqueline and I can never be. Kerry is the woman who has my heart, I wouldn't have married her if I didn't truly love her."

"I know, buddy, and I'm pretty sure she feels the same way about you," said Matt as a tall middle-aged blond caught his attention. He soon lost interest as he watched her crawl across the stage on all fours, he knew he had something better waiting for him at home.

They had their last round of drinks, and like the waitress had said, instead of adding to the crazies that were already on the road, they called a cab to take them home, and thanks to AAA, Matt's car was towed to his home free of charge.

CHAPTER 19

Droves of parents were on full alert as the students of Alexander Shaw High School made their exit—the school's full-lockdown had just been lifted. Some of the students were still visibly shaken as they rushed to be beside their parents after the extensive ordeal.

The school's administration was contacted by an anonymous tipster and made aware of a burgundy Toyota Lexus that kept circling the school. Once security was informed, part of the school's policy was that they go immediately into full-scale lockdown. Whenever there were children involved, taking any risks was out of the question.

Kerry stood on her tiptoes as she placed herself between the truck and the driver side door in desperate search of Ke'Auna, whom hadn't returned any of her text messages in the past three hours. She figured her daughter's phone must have died, otherwise she would have responded immediately.

Kerry felt guilty. Although she had good intentions, she never got around to telling Ke'Auna about the strange wine-colored car, possibly a

Toyota Lexus, hanging around their home, just a few days prior. The possibility was imminent that it was the same vehicle that was circling the school—burgundy and wine-colored are two different ways to describe the same color—both cars were also said to have the same dark tinted windows. The similarities were too immense to be a coincidence. Kerry was certain it was the same car. The driver just had to be identified.

She spotted her daughter trotting between two other groups of girls, twisting her body from side to side to not bump into anyone, her best friend Heather was right by her side. "Ke'Auna, Heather. Over here!" she yelled, frantically waving her arm, she felt relieved when they spotted her.

Kerry watched as the girls hopped inside the truck; Ke'Auna took the front seat, Heather took the back, she immediately climbed behind the wheel and began asking questions. "So, what's everybody panicked about?" she said, quizzically.

"They said the school sent out text alerts to all students about someone lurking around the school, but since both of our phones are dead, we didn't get any messages, but I did read the message off someone else's phone," Ke'Auna said as she fastened her seatbelt, then grabbed a mirror from her purse to check her lip gloss.

The parents had also received text messages from the school so Kerry knew full well what was happening, she just wanted to find out how much the girls knew. "I never got a response back from any of my texts to you either, so I figured your phone must have died. I just wanted to make sure you were okay."

Heather remained quiet during the trip home. She paid close attention as Kerry expressed her concern for Ke'Auna and wondered if her mom received the same text message and if so, why weren't she at the school to pick her up? Her concerns were answered as soon as they pulled into the driveway.

"Heather, make sure you call your mom and tell her you're okay. I spoke to her earlier and she's worried sick."

"Okay, Mrs. Gaines," said Heather, elated to hear of her mom's concern.

Ke'Auna stood at the front of her mom's truck and watched her friend ease down the driveway, her head held high as her long beautiful black hair laid perfectly on her back, it was straight and flat as if it had been pressed. She's always admired Heather's long chemical-free hair, and wished she had hair like that of her own. "Talk to you later, girl."

Heather didn't bother turning around when she said, "Later."

Kerry waited for her daughter to enter the house before shutting the front door, then told her about the incident that took place a few days prior, involving the burgundy or wine-colored Lexus, the intentions of the driver was precarious, but she told her daughter to be on alert.

Ke'Auna went inside her bedroom and closed the door, then laid across the bed and shut her eyes, they flew back open almost instantly.

The doorbell was followed by three hard knocks, catching all three family members completely off guard. Ke'Auna just listened as she laid still.

Kerry, who had just extracted a chicken from the freezer and placed it inside the sink so that it could be thawed out by dinner, heard her husband mumble what sounded like an expletive as he came up the hallway, he was clearly irritated from the loud knocks. As far as she knew, they weren't expecting any visitors, and even if they were, no one would show up at the front door of their safe haven being so unruly and disrespectful, so they already knew that whoever was at the door was unknown to them.

Kevin pulled open the door and saw some familiar faces. The majority of them were guys he'd worked with for years—he thought it was a celebratory moment, letting him know he was coming back to work, until Lieutenant White stepped forward, waving a document in the air.

"Kevin Gaines, I have a warrant for your arrest."

"What! Are you kidding me?"

"I'm afraid I'm not, sir."

"For what this time?"

"The murder of Shane Forbes," said the lieutenant. "I'm following orders, sir."

Kevin looked over his shoulder and noticed his wife standing near the entryway to the kitchen. She didn't utter a word, the tears streaming down her face spoke volumes.

"I don't know what's going on, baby. Be strong for me and take care of our daughter," he said as he turned around and allowed himself to be placed in cuffs, then walked to the cruiser with his head down.

The ordeal he thought was ending was just getting started, and only time would tell if he had what it took to withstand it?

CHAPTER 20

Kevin Gaines had never in his life woke up to such deplorable conditions. A strong stench of raw urine filled both of his nostrils, causing a deep burn in his nasal passages. Ventilation inside the cell was slim to none. A sharp pain was eminent in his lower back as he tried to sit up. After a couple of attempts, he decided it was best to remain on his back. *Fuck!* he said to himself when reality sunk in. He glanced at the stainless steel sink/toilet combo mounted to the wall a few feet away from his bed, the inside of the toilet was a dark-greenish color, he assumed it was the source of the foul stench.

The makeshift bed was a long slab of metal that was hard on his entire body. He had a difficult time falling asleep the night before. He laid there for hours, thinking about his wife and daughter, hoping they were holding up well and not worrying about him too much, until suddenly, everything went blank. He often woke up during the night when he slept at home, usually because Kerry would press her ample backside into his crotch as she changed sleeping positions, the thought alone stirred something deep within his loins—there wasn't anything he wouldn't do to get back to her.

He managed to roll out of the hard unyielding bed to brush his teeth. The super low-budget toothpaste was ineffective and left a strange dry taste in his mouth, no matter how many times he gargled and swished hot water around in his mouth, he couldn't rid himself of the unpleasant taste.

He picked up a bible that sat at the foot of his bed. The top of the page told him he was in the book of Revelation, and he silently prayed that he hadn't reached his end?

He leaned on his elbow as he began to read. It had been years since he'd picked up a bible, or any religious book for that matter, and if he hadn't been in such a vulnerable position, he was certain he still wouldn't have picked it up.

It didn't take him long to get lost in his reading. He had four filthy walls surrounding him with no distractions. From afar, he heard keys dangling here and there from guards that were moving around, but from the moment he was brought in the evening before, he hadn't seen or heard another inmate, so he wondered how many others, if any, were in the vicinity? He was in a section of the jail known as protective custody. Since he was an ex-police officer, and possibly the reason why other inmates were in custody, he had to be kept separate from general population. Coming in contact with other prisoners could have easily cost him his life—unless he was suicidal, the only way to keep him safe was to keep him by himself—he prayed his ordeal would be over soon.

He had been reading for about an hour when he heard keys. The sound became louder and louder as they got closer to his cell. "Mr. Gaines?" an officer said when he reached the door. "Are you Gaines?"

"Yes," he said as he stared at him through the door's narrow window, the awkward way he was lying made him sit up straight, he couldn't help but wince as a sharp pain shot through his back.

"Here's your breakfast, sir. We almost forgot you were back here," the officer said. "Push your door open when you hear it click."

The ex-lieutenant hopped off the bunk and reached his cell door as soon as it clicked. He pushed the door open and grabbed the plastic tray he was handed. He looked down at what appeared to be scrambled eggs, corn-flakes, and a slice of cake—a single carton of milk sat atop. "Thank you."

"You're welcome, sir," said the officer. "Let me know if you need anything; books, newspapers, magazines, or whatever. I'm sure it could prob-ably get pretty lonely down here."

"Okay," said Kevin before the cell door shut. He regretted not getting the officer's name, he was glad to be treated with some form of respect. *Next time* he thought.

It was somewhere between nine-thirty and a quarter to ten. He had consumed his breakfast and had dozed off, when his cell door began clicking, jarring him awake. "Mr. Gaines, cell eighteen!" he heard an officer yell. "Get dressed and come out; you have an attorney visit."

He exited his cell and saw an officer standing in front of the module, waiting for him. He walked to him and was pointed to a staircase just a few feet outside of the module's front door, he quickly ascended the stairs two steps at a time, and was greeted by another officer at the top of the stairs. "Name please," the officer said.

"Gaines. Kevin Gaines."

"Mr. Gaines, your attorney is waiting for you in the first room to your right," he said as he pulled a door open for him, exposing a hallway that led to six rooms. "Come back out through this door when your visit concludes."

"Yep," said Kevin. He entered the hallway and went into the small room he was directed to, and saw a healthy black woman awaiting him. Her face was mediocre—her plus-size body was doable, he thought, but each of her arms were literally the size of his thighs.

"Mr. Gaines?"

"Yes," he said, hoping for good news.

"Mr. Gaines, my name is Juanita Howard. I'm an attorney from the Police Union. I was sent to represent you in your murder case."

"Okay," he said reluctantly. "Nice to meet you, Miss Howard."

"Nice to meet you too, I wish it was under better circumstances," she said.

"Sure would've been nice," he said as he took a seat. "Have you been provided the facts of the case?"

"I have," she said quickly. "I can tell you right now it doesn't look good."

He was alarmed by her response, and was unsure of what to say next.

"You're scheduled to make your first court appearance tomorrow morning, of which you'll be asked to enter a plea. How do you plan to plea, Mr. Gaines?"

Her entire demeanor seemed off to him. Her body language alone told him she didn't have his best interest at heart, every minute that went by made him more uncomfortable. "Not guilty, Miss Howard."

"That's what I was afraid of," she said while looking down. "I understand you have a wife and daughter?" she said as she raised her head to look him squarely in the eyes.

He shifted when he spoke, becoming more uncomfortable. "I do."

"Do you really want to put them through this, Mr.Gaines? I mean, from what I read the state has a rock-solid case against you. It would be a slam-dunk win for the prosecutor if you decide to take this case to trial."

"Do you have the discovery?"

"I don't, not yet," she said quickly. "A discovery won't be prepared until after you enter a plea, but I was contacted by the DA's office this morning and they offered a deal. You should really consider taking it to make it easier on your family," she said as if she personally knew his loved ones.

He had no interest in accepting a plea bargain, but he wanted to hear what she had to say. "What's the offer?"

"They're offering you a one to six if you plead to involuntary manslaughter."

"Wow," he said, seemingly surprised. "Miss Howard, how long have you worked for the Police Union?"

"Ten years."

"In your ten years, have you ever seen a case where a deal like mine was offered?"

"It's common, Mr. Gaines. I've never had a case where a deal was offered before discovery or a plea was entered, but because you're an ex-lieutenant for the department, I'm sure that has a lot to do with it. I personally think it's a great offer."

"Maybe too great, don't you think?"

She looked at him without answering.

"Miss Howard, they know as well as I do that no crime was committed, that's also the reason they're offering me a deal so soon. Did you read the case?"

"Of course I read it," she said.

"If you read it I don't see why you didn't turn the offer down as soon as they offered it. You would know that they have no case if you'd read it correctly."

"That's an insult, Mr. Gaines."

"No, you coming down here to visit me is an insult, Miss Howard. They played you and you don't even see it," he told her bluntly. "How many white officers have you represented, Miss Howard?"

"Plenty."

"White officers who were accused of killing an unarmed black person?"

"None."

"Exactly, that's because none were ever charged," he said. "But because I'm black and accused of killing an unarmed white person, they send a black woman down here to try to convince me to cop out to an incident that wasn't a crime. I was preserving my own life in the line of duty."

"So, you don't want the deal?"

"Fuck no! I don't want you coming down here to see me no more either," he said as he stood, then left the room.

Juanita Howard was shocked. She sat there for a while feeling feeble-minded, replaying in her head everything that was said, then slowly stood from the table and made her exit. She was taken aback. She had never before had a client be so rude to her.

CHAPTER 21

Ex-metro lieutenant Kevin Gaines entered District Court's Department sixteen dressed in wrinkled-navy blue jail garbs as opposed to the creased down policeman uniform he was accustomed to, accompanied by belly-chains and leg shackles, severely restricting his movement.

He peered around the courtroom, looking for his wife, and became somewhat disappointed when he didn't see her. He'd been allowed a phone call and a shower the evening before, so he explained to Kerry what was on the horizon. He wouldn't have known about his court date if it hadn't been for Juanita Howard from the Police Union, whose first impression told him she was a dump truck attorney, but for the heads up, he was thankful she'd come.

He sensed the anger in his wife's voice when he explained their visit. She on the other hand told him she'd notify Summer and tell her what was up, and without his knowledge, a plan was hatched.

He saw a lot of unfamiliar faces as he was escorted by a jail officer to a table on the left side of Judge Mitchell Fields' courtroom—the only person sitting there was Juanita Howard.

"Good morning, Mr. Gaines," she said with a smile that he knew was fake.

He was still simmering over the exchange of words they engaged in the day before, so he offered a similar fake grin and said, "Good morning." He hadn't seen his wife when she made her entrance. She came in and sat in the corner near the rear of the courtroom, sitting beside her, was Summer Sinclair.

The bailiff instructed the courtroom to rise then told them all to be seated after a couple of seconds.

Judge Fields stood about six feet eight inches tall. He didn't just have long lower extremities, but his torso was long and so was his neck, so even after he sat behind the bench, he was still towering. "This is the only matter I have on the calendar this morning and it's a rather serious case, do both sides think you're ready to go forward?"

"Judge, my client was brought in literally just a few minutes ago, would it be okay if I had a few minutes with him?"

Judge Fields didn't give an answer. He crossed his arms and looked toward the prosecutor, of whom he already knew was ready to oppose.

"Judge, Miss Howard had plenty of time to confer with her client," said the short pudgy district attorney. "In fact, she had all day yesterday to speak with him. If she failed to do so, then that's too bad."

Judge Fields gave the prosecutor a half-hearted smile. He didn't understand why the man was so on edge. "Counselor, this is nothing to argue about. She simply asked for a few minutes to speak with her client, I personally don't see any harm in that?"

"Judge, we offered a deal in this case. The state would simply like to know if it was accepted by the defendant, or if we need to go ahead and prepare this case for trial?"

Juanita Howard rose quickly and tried to contain her anger as she spoke directly to the prosecutor. "If you keep your mouth shut for a few minutes while I speak to Mr. Gaines, we can all find out together whether or not he wants the deal."

The judge banged his gavel and demanded order. "Speak to me, counselor, don't go picking a fight with the prosecutor," he said while looking directly at her. "Both sides can make all the objections they want, it's how the courts work, but I'm the one who decides what happens or doesn't happen inside my courtroom. I won't tolerate any ignorance, is that understood?"

"It is, judge," she said, appearing to calm down.

"Good," replied Judge Fields. "Go ahead and have a few minutes with your client, Miss Howard. I had no idea a plea deal had already been offered. A plea hasn't even been entered yet. In fact, how do you plea to the charge of second-degree murder, Mr. Gaines?"

"Not guilty, Your Honor," he said immediately.

The prosecutor had no comment.

Juanita Howard leaned inward and whispered to her client, "Mr. Gaines, it's clear from the meeting we had yesterday that you and I are probably not the best suited."

Kevin Gaines nodded in agreement but didn't say anything.

"We can't say it's a conflict of interest just because we had a disagreement. Lawyers and clients don't always agree, nor get along, it's just how it is, but it doesn't constitute a conflict of interest. Are you following what I'm saying?"

"I'm trying," he said honestly.

"This is the tactic I think you should use," she began in a whisper. "Like I said yesterday, I've never seen a case where a deal was offered before a plea was entered. To me, that suggests that there may be trouble with the State's case against you. I could be wrong so don't quote me on that."

"You think it's suspicious though?"

"Very," she said with her brows raised.

"I didn't do anything wrong, Miss Howard, that's what I was trying to tell you yesterday," he told her. "So, what do I do?"

"I think you should request to represent yourself in this case."

He looked at her sadly and said, "You're playing, right?"

"I'm serious."

"Why would I do something that stupid, I'm not a lawyer!"

"You're not requesting it to represent yourself for real, Mr. Gaines," she said in a voice that was comforting to him. "It's a strategic move. If you ask to represent yourself and the judge grants it, the state, by law, would have to provide you with the discovery in its entirety. You'll know exactly what kind of evidence they have against you, if any, and you'll be able to make a rational decision on whether it'll be in your best interest to take a deal, or go to trial."

Judge Fields couldn't believe it when he heard the request. Neither could the prosecutor.

"Mr. Gaines, this case involves some complex issues. Do you have any experience in dealing with law?"

"No."

"Have you ever attended law school or anything like that?"

"No."

"After the brief canvass, it's the court's opinion, based on the answers provided, that you're not qualified to deal with the issues competently," explained the judge.

"You're probably right, judge, but I'd rather take my chances on defending myself opposed to handing my future over to Miss Howard here," replied the ex-lieutenant.

"It's the court's discretion on whether or not a defendant is capable, competent, or qualified enough to represent himself, and I don't think you're qualified. Not even remotely. I'm sorry, Mr. Gaines, but your request is denied," the judge told him.

Summer Sinclair walked up the aisle, slowly, filled with confidence, looking as sexy as ever, everyone turned to look at her when she began speaking. "Judge Fields, I don't think it'll be necessary for me to introduce myself since you and I are already very well acquainted."

"We are indeed, Mrs. Sinclair," replied the judge. "But, what is your business in this case, counselor?"

"Well, you just denied Mr. Gaines' request to represent himself in this courtroom, and you and I both know that Miss Howard's representation would be severely inadequate."

"How would you know when I never got a chance to represent him— let's not go there?" Juanita Howard spat sharply from the defendant's table.

Summer quickly turned toward the Police Union's attorney and diffused the situation before Judge Fields saw a reason to intervene. "Miss Howard, being present and sitting next to Mr. Gaines in court does not equal adequate representation. I don't have anything against you per se, but all lawyers from the Police Union are full of it. I'm sure you know that as well as I do?"

"Talk to me, counselor. Don't insult Miss Howard or anyone else inside my courtroom," the judge said from the bench. "Again, what is your business in this case, Mrs. Sinclair?"

"Your Honor, I'm representing Mr. Gaines in these proceedings from this point on," she said as she and the judge made eye contact.

"Are you asking me or telling me, Mrs. Sinclair?"

"Judge, I'm not trying to make a big fuss about it, but I'm requesting to be made the attorney of record."

The judge reclined in his seat, and peered at the bailiff, seemingly amused. "To appease the court, Mrs. Sinclair, why all of a sudden you want to be the attorney of record? I mean, is there a personal interest; do you know the defendant?"

"I do know the defendant. I know him quite well, actually," said Mrs. Sinclair. "More specifically, Mr. Gaines is the best friend of my husband Matt. His wife Kerry, who is in the audience, is my best friend, our daughters Ke'Auna and Heather are besties as well."

"Isn't that a conflict of some sort?" the judge asked.

"I believe it is," the prosecutor interjected.

"I checked and it's not," answered Mrs. Sinclair. "There's no law anywhere on the books that says I can't represent someone simply because I know them."

"Let's say that's true, Mrs. Sinclair," the judge began.

"It is, I'm telling you I checked."

"I believe you, but there's still something I need to know," said Judge Fields. "If I make a determination and decide that you are suitable to be Mr. Gaines' attorney of record, are you asking to be appointed so that you can bill this court, or are you asking to take this case pro bono?"

Summer Sinclair looked down at the floor, then at Mr. Gaines, then turned toward the audience to look at Kerry. She knew it would cost a substantial amount of money to represent Kevin Gaines in a zealous manner. She also knew that she couldn't afford to foot such a bill herself, and if she asked to be appointed so she could bill the court, she would be risking having the case taken away from her. She also wanted to see to it that her best friend's husband would be treated fairly by a system that she knew was prejudice. She looked up at the judge and said, "Pro bono."

"That's fair enough, Mrs. Sinclair," the judge said. "Your request to be counsel for Kevin Gaines is hereby granted. Your request to do it pro bono is also granted. You're relieved of your duties in this case, Miss Howard. The defense' representation in this case has been handed over to Attorney Summer Sinclair."

"Judge, I also request a gag order be issued in this case. We don't need this turning into a media circus," Summer said, professionally.

"Objection, Your Honor," said the district attorney. "This case has already been highly publicized. The press should still be allowed to cover the outcome."

"Gag order granted. I don't want any cameras inside my courtroom, however, whatever they cover outside those doors is not my business," the judge said before slamming his gavel.

CHAPTER 22

Crowds took to the streets again in protest. This time they gathered in front of the Regional Justice Center in downtown Vegas. Not because of the premature shooting death of nineteen-year-old Shane Forbes, but, the protesters were upset at, not only the criminal justice system, but at Criminal Defense Attorney Summer Sinclair for volunteering to defend the officer who shot the unarmed man.

No one understood why a very decent-looking, respectable, professional white woman would come to the aid of a man with a polarized complexion, when the believed-to-be-innocent victim in the case was a pigment almost identical to hers?

Judge Fields, the presiding judge, was brought to the forefront every time either party filed something that had to be addressed by the court. This time the motion had come from the defendant's end. "I put a lot of thought into this motion you filed for bail, Mrs. Sinclair."

She acknowledged the statement with a nod of her head, but didn't take her eyes off of him as he continued speaking.

"The law states that a fair and impartial hearing must be provided by the presiding judge, in any instance, where an officer of the law is facing a serious offense."

"I think this qualifies as one of those instances, judge," said the beautiful, sensational Summer Sinclair, her dark shiny black hair oozing loads of sex appeal.

"I happen to agree with you, counselor," replied Judge Fields as he peered up at her over the rim of his expensive-looking glasses. "I think a reasonable bail is ten thousand?"

"We'll happily take that, judge. Thank you," said Summer.

The D.A. appeared as though he was considering objecting to what he thought was a low blow to the prosecution, but instead of opposing, he threw his hands in the air and submitted to it.

Summer looked down at Kevin and smiled as she stood next to him.

He looked up at her and returned the gesture. "See you soon," he told her.

"I look forward to it," she said, turning on her heels to exit the courtroom.

Four hours later, the twosome found themselves cozied up together in a heart-shaped vibrating bed inside of a honeymoon suite at the Rio Hotel.

"This ass looks so good and it's so hot," Kevin said as he admired her rear assets, using his hands to squeeze her plump soft cheeks before running his hot wet tongue up and down its crack, then took the time to lick around and all over her puckering asshole. "You taste so delicious, baby."

"Your tongue feels so good, Kevin. You might make me come if you keep doing that. Ooooh, it feels sooo gooood," she whispered.

Her black stallion continued to lash his tongue up and down her backside, she moaned and pushed back, wiggling and grinding her asshole hard against his tongue, showing him how much she was enjoying it. She reached back with one hand and pushed down on his head, forcing his face even deeper into her hot ass crack, as she tooted up her butt to give his mouth more access. She then slid her other hand underneath her body, and in-between her legs to rub her swollen clit, she played with herself until she reached orgasm.

Her lover let his tongue slide smoothly from her asshole to her sopping vagina. He licked her clitoris aggressively, sucked it, blew on it to tease it, and then licked it some more before thrusting his tongue deeply inside of her to taste and savor her delicious juices.

"My god, Kevin. Fuck!" she said, clearly out of breath. "Fuck me with your tongue."

She got no verbal response, but his actions made her arch her back even more.

She felt his hands spreading her ass cheeks apart as he resumed getting his fill of her throbbing hot asshole.

"Oh my god, Kevin. Mmmm. Mmm. Oohh yesss!"

"Your asshole is so hot and tasty, baby," he said between licks. "I bet if I sat some kernels of popcorn on it right now those motherfuckers would pop," he said humorously.

She smiled but not for long. She felt his large hard penis slide up the inside of her thigh then on her ass cheek as he mounted her. His endowment first penetrated her wet vagina as deep as he could push as she lie on her stomach, then before she knew it, he plunged it deep and hard inside of her asshole and began to fuck her as if there was no tomorrow. She loved it. He fucked her the way she needed to be—she found herself hoping it would never stop.

CHAPTER 23

From a distance and under the safety and security of the cubbyhole he called his office, Chief Dunlap kept a watchful eye on the case that continued to ruffle the feathers of thousands of Las Vegans. He kept a tentative ear available to the radio to stay abreast of everything that happened—reinforcements were already on standby in case they were needed.

There were many disturbances all over the valley, mostly non-violent, but on occasion, there were some clashes when different groups of protesters came in contact with supporters from the opposing side—one incident that happened in front of a marijuana dispensary sent two stabbing victims to trauma for immediate surgery. One person was arrested and charged with two counts of attempted murder.

Chief Dunlap saw to it that the department was braced and ready for whatever happened, there was no telling when someone might decide to get ignorant, he thought.

He watched his officers segregate themselves inside the precinct. White officers ate lunch together, as well as the blacks, and in instances where there were black and white teams who patrolled the streets together, he'd received numerous requests on his desk, literally from every bi-racial duo, asking to be partnered with someone of the same race. A lot of swapping took place as he honored their requests—it looked like Jim Crow all over again.

Chief Dunlap sat watching CNN on his tablet, what was happening in Las Vegas scrolled across the ticker on the bottom of the screen. He also watched some of the coverage on different local news channels—each of the anchors added their own spin—but it was close in proximity even with the different perspectives.

He nodded his head in shame as he thought about the chaos. In his heart of hearts, he knew Mayor Kason was responsible for it. *All of this to keep my job* he thought. His temper began to flare as he continued thinking. *If I'd just stuck to my guns and did what I knew was right, none of this would be happening.* He knew that it was highly unlikely to predict the future, but once everything came to pass and the smoke settled, he hoped to be able to say it was all worth it? That's the only way he'd be able to forgive himself.

CHAPTER 24

The thermometer read ninety-six degrees when Matthew Sinclair pulled it from his daughter's mouth. It was ninety-nine when he checked it an hour earlier, so he was beyond elated to see that her fever had begun to come down. He used his index finger to remove the long strand of glossy black hair from her face. It was thick and saturated, and he couldn't be sure if the wetness had come from her sweating profusely, or from the cool-wet rag he'd placed on her forehead. Nonetheless, the cause was the least of his worries, he was just grateful to see that his little princess was getting better.

He held the chilled glass of orange juice to her quivering mouth and encouraged her to take a small sip. "Great job, kiddo. Here, drink some more, it's going to make you feel a lot better."

Heather struggled, but managed to take another sip, then another, and another...she continued to do so until the glass was empty.

Matthew flashed her a grin before kissing her forehead. "You know sweetheart, for someone who wants to be a nurse, it sure looks like you're having a great time being a patient."

She smiled shyly and lowered her chin to her chest.

"It's okay, sweetie. Mommy and I are going to get you better. I know you feel crappy, but it's important that you eat when she brings you breakfast."

Heather shook her head no.

"Please, baby. Just eat a little bit. Can you do that for papa...please?"

She hesitated a bit, and then shook her head yes.

"Thank you," he said before kissing her forehead again.

Summer came into her daughter's bedroom, carrying a plate and another small glass of orange juice.

"Mommy's here with your breakfast, sweetheart. Remember you promised me that you'll eat some," her dad said.

"How's my baby?" Summer said as she sat beside her on the bed, holding the plate in her hand while sitting the glass of orange juice on the nightstand next to the bed.

"Her temperature came down three degrees, and she did drink a whole glass of orange juice," her husband told her.

"That's great," said Summer. "Mommy's here now baby. I got your favorite breakfast...scrambled eggs and oatmeal. I need you to eat some of it for me, okay?"

Heather didn't say anything. She opened her mouth, inviting her mom to feed her.

"That's good, sweetie. I'm so proud of you," Summer said as Heather ingested a spoonful of oatmeal, filled with melted butter and sugar the way she loved it. "Isn't that good, sweetheart? Here, how 'bout some more?"

They'd spent the evening before at the Painted Desert Park, a place they went to on occasion to spend time as a family, it was when they returned home, they noticed her fever.

"Okay, princess, time to rest," her dad told her before helping her under the covers and tucking her in.

They both gave her a kiss on the cheek before leaving her bedroom.

"So, what's on the agenda for today?" Matt asked Summer.

"The same old shuck and jive," said Summer. "I keep getting hounded by the D.A.'s office about my client that absconded. They swear up and down that I know where he is—like I'm hiding him or something."

"Is that the Ray guy you mentioned before?"

"That's the one. Raymar Ray is wherever he is. Only he knows," said Summer.

"I wouldn't worry about it," her husband told her.

"I'm not…so, what would you like for breakfast this morning?"

Matthew smiled as he pondered her question. He tried to hide it when she looked at him.

"What's so funny?"

"Your question about breakfast," he told her.

"I asked what you'd like to eat, what's funny about that? Are you trying to say you don't like my cooking?"

"No, I'm not saying that at all—what I want is already done, and it's hot," he said with a sneer.

Summer smiled as she caught on to what he was saying. She stopped in her tracks and started pulling down her pajamas, and then her panties. She pulled off her shirt and said, "I can handle that."

"Not here," said Matt as he picked her clothes up from the floor and ushered her to their bedroom, holding her arm.

The downward dog position was one she was no stranger to. After a day, mostly spent going over different theories and strategies with her investigator Gerald Osby, Summer Sinclair wanted to relieve some built-up tension and unwanted stress, so she attended an all-female Piyo class at the gym after work, but she hadn't anticipated being the center of attention. She noticed several female spectators checking her out as they gathered behind her in the back of the class. She was used to being complimented by women, admiring her figure, so she continued to stretch, aligning her back with her legs until the top of her head settled comfortably on the floor between her feet, her hands remained fixed to her waist as the ascension began until she was upright. She knew that she was in a class that was filled with comely women, so she didn't understand why all of the attention was on her—some of the other women were drop-dead gorgeous.

She wore a pair of dark pink yoga pants that had been pulled from store shelves nationwide for its sheer material, but because she had on a pair of panties to match, she assumed it wouldn't be as noticeable, but she came to realize how wrong she was.

She had only been stretching for twenty minutes when she began to perspire. It's also around the time when she began to feel the thin fabric cutting deeply into the crevice of her ample backside, but with so many unwanted observers having her under a microscope, she was too embarrassed to reach back and pull them out. She decided to let them be for the time being, but, of course, as long as they stayed in a forbidden place, the ladies would continue to stare, making her more uncomfortable, so she grabbed her belongings and ended her session.

Normally she took a quick shower before leaving the gym, but this time she waited until she got home. She'd often heard women complain about receiving ravenous looks from men, she could relate because she'd received them herself, but she knew nothing compared to what she'd just experienced. Her husband took her into his arms to console her when she explained it to him.

The loud-chilling scream cut through the stillness of darkness like the deafening sound of a gunshot blast inside of a small enclosure.

"Help! Nooo! Donnn't!...Stoppp!"

The fear-gripping scream startled both Kevin and Kerry, shaking them violently awake from a deep death-like sleep, the only thing they could think of was their daughter Ke'Auna.

"Baby, what's going on?" Kerry said frantically as she lie beside her husband, fully out of her slumber, her sensitive senses severely heightened.

"I don't know, but that was our baby," he said as he scrambled out of bed.

As soon as the bedroom door burst open, Ke'Auna, who appeared to be panic-stricken as she sat frozen on the floor beside her bed, stood up and darted into her father's arms. "Daddy, I'm scared," she said in her softest voice.

"You're okay now, baby. Daddy's here," said Kevin as he released his grip and gave her a onceover to make sure she was okay before running hastily to the open window inside of her bedroom. He saw a medium sized figure jumping over the fence from inside his yard, wearing all black attire before slipping into the driver's seat of a dark-colored car. It immediately scurried off after the door slammed. He wasn't certain, but he thought it was the same vehicle that had been seen a couple of times by his wife and neighbor hanging around their street, and also spotted lurking around Alexander Shaw High School, it was too dark for him to pay attention to any detail. He returned to his daughter's side who was being consoled by her mom.

"She's okay, baby. I got her," Kerry said while kneeling on the floor holding Ke'Auna to her bosom, gently rubbing her back as she rocked back and forth. She stared at her husband in a manner as if she expected him to start providing answers.

"Who the hell is in that car?" he said, thinking aloud.

"What car?" said Kerry.

"I think it was the burgundy Lexus, I'm not sure?"

No more words were spoken for quite some time. The mention of the burgundy car was a shocking revelation, for weeks everyone inside the household had been on the lookout for it.

"The bastard intruded my home?" Kerry said in a whisper. Her gaze focused on her daughter as she eyed her closely, her nightclothes still appeared to be in decent shape, and besides the window being open, nothing else inside the bedroom seemed to have been disturbed. "Baby, did he say anything—did he touch you?"

"She grabbed me and told me to come with her, but she wasn't trying to hurt me."

"She…a woman?" her dad asked.

"Sounded like it," Ke'Auna said.

Kevin and Kerry just looked at each other. What would a woman want with their daughter, they wondered? Kevin went and grabbed his phone from its charger and called in a complaint, and was told by the dispatcher that the police would be there shortly.

Fifteen minutes later, two officers arrived—the ex-lieutenant knew them personally. Almost immediately after they showed up on scene, he noticed that they both seemed disinterested about the intrusion—they asked no relevant questions in regards to the incident, and they never once asked if Ke'Auna was okay. He really wasn't surprised, being that they weren't the only two officers who'd turned on him, but it bothered him to know that they had no interest in protecting a child, especially one as beautiful and innocent as Ke'Auna. The two men he once referred to as his brothers made him very uncomfortable—he wanted them out of his house as quickly as possible—he would have never turned on them the way they did him, the sooner they left, the better, he thought.

All the while, he was troubled by the fact that the intruder was a woman. What kind of woman out there had the balls to enter his home?

The Oceanblue Estates were not as safe as they once were—everyone who lived in the housing development was on edge.

CHAPTER 25

Private Investigator Gerald Osby pulled slowly into the parking lot of the strip mall on Warm Springs and Rainbow. Unfortunately, it was the same corner Shane Forbes' life was snatched. His supervisor Summer Sinclair sent him to see what he could dig up.

He looked around the scenery, trying to get a mental picture of what happened on the day Shane Forbes was pronounced deceased. He tried to get a visual of how many passersby were on scene, and how everyone had probably panicked when the shot rang out.

He brought his vehicle to a slow creep as he swerved into a parking space in front of the Moneytree next door to Starbucks—adjacent to that, was the Cricket Store. From what he understood, Summer had already spoken to a credible witness who happened to be an employee of the store, and was on shift the day Shane Forbes was killed. The employee/witness' name was Belinda Hopkins.

Belinda had examined the store's surveillance footage over and over, looking at different shots from a multitude of angles, hoping to find something no one else had noticed, to see if there was any justification for all the protests. Truth was, there was no footage from any of the store's surveillance that showed what happened inside of the parking lot before or during the shooting. Shane's death was the end result, but it did show footage of him inside of the store walking around aimlessly and erratically, hand inside of his shirt with his finger protruding as if he was pointing a concealed weapon, resembling a six-year-old child playing a game of Cowboys and Indians.

"Looks like he's on some kind of drug," the investigator said.

"I don't know," said Belinda. "I keep my opinions to myself, there seems to be enough of those already. I see no sense in adding to it."

"Can't refute that," the investigator said embarrassed, wishing he hadn't voiced his personal opinion. He turned his attention back to the surveillance. Even from the store's camera perception, anyone that saw it could have easily mistaken the pointed finger to be a weapon.

The investigator had been instructed by his boss to retrieve the tapes so that they could be used as evidence when or if the case went to trial. Their thoughts were, if the surveillance from inside of the store ever saw the light of day, it would clearly explain why the call was reported as an armed robbery, and it would justify why the ex-lieutenant arrived on the scene expecting to come face to face with an armed person, and that he had every right to presume the man was armed and dangerous.

Investigator Gerald Osby left the Moneytree, satisfied with what he'd retrieved. He then went to Metro's 911 Emergency Dispatch Center and obtained a copy of the phone call made by Belinda Hopkins from inside the store during the robbery attempt—their case was coming along nicely, he thought.

He knew his boss would be content when he showed her what he had. He texted her to tell her that he was headed back to the office, for the life of him, he couldn't understand why the evidence he possessed hadn't been collected by metro or provided to any of the news medias? Sloppy police work was the only thing that could explain it, but he was thankful for their incompetence.

CHAPTER 26

Ke'Auna and Heather's game of dress-up ended before it started. They had just entered Heather's bedroom when they heard the car's squealing, street-hugging, high-performance sounding tires sliding across the asphalt as they fought to grasp for traction on the dimly-lit street of Beech Family.

In a split-second, the teenage girls were in the bedroom window at the Sinclair residence, looking to see who was burning so much rubber, a sound that was rarely heard in that area, the closest they had personally ever come to hearing it was when they watched TV. They witnessed the burgundy Toyota finally get the traction it had been trying so hard to get, and peel down the street in what seemed like a hurry.

Seconds later, Kevin Gaines shot from behind a parked car in front of his home. He figured the driver of the Toyota must have spotted him when he ducked in between the two vehicles, he had only been seconds away from finding out who the driver was.

He was on his way next door to pick up his daughter when he saw the car sitting stationary in the shadows of his neighbor's house across the street. He was contemplating on whether or not he should approach it in an attempt to identify the driver when it began moving forward—he regretted it instantly for not spotting it sooner, or perhaps, he could have moved a little swifter and may have went unnoticed—but neither here nor there, he still didn't know who was intentionally stalking his family. Normally, his first reaction would be to call the police, but they'd already shown that he'd be wasting his time.

Ke'Auna came out of the house with Heather in tow. Summer was closely behind making sure Ke'Auna got safely into her father's arms, a safety precaution both families practiced.

Summer and Kevin made eye contact when he took his daughter graciously into his arms and wrapped her up in a warm embrace.

Summer gave a nod as she smiled at him. She yearned to be in his massive arms again, and found herself wondering how much longer it would be before it happened? Her body was aching to feel the pain mixed with pleasure she experienced each time they got together—her vaginal canal began to throb and sop with juices as she thought of him giving her mountains of pleasure.

She wondered if he was sexually content after spending time with his wife—it was their night of the month to have some alone time, however, she would have much rather that it had been with her, because although Matt's performance had been less than mediocre the past few times they had sex, she needed to be dominated and satisfied sexually the way Kevin was known to do it, and she hoped it was something that would soon come to pass. Her insides ached with anticipation.

CHAPTER 27

Las Vegas was the fastest growing city in America. Millions of people called it their home, but it was constantly growing, becoming home to thousands of others, each day, each week, each month and each year, construction on every other corner, it was constantly revolving and reinventing itself, making itself much better and more enticing, building structures all over the place, whether it be a building, a highway, byway or a sewage canal, something always seemed to be under construction. Brick by brick, piece by piece, layer by layer is how all of the structures were put together—District Attorney Tom Hardy built his cases the same way.

He just wanted to convict a man just because an unarmed one of his people had been gunned down. He didn't give a shit if he was guilty or not, but ex-lieutenant Kevin Gaines was in his grips, and he had no intention of letting him go, neither peacefully or otherwise.

He wanted someone to pay, period! His thoughts were, Shane Forbes could have been his kid, his kid's friend, his nephew, or one of his buddy's child, or even his next door neighbor, and for that reason, he was prepared to convict, and not bend for any reason towards offering another plea bargain— he wanted to literally take away the life of the one he thought was guilty of the slaying—ex-lieutenant Gaines. He had him in his throes, he wanted him so bad he could taste him. He just wanted to hear the jury speak those words of guilt. A reading of *guilty* by the jury's foreperson from the verdict form would be music to his ears. He could taste blood as he thought of such an accomplishment.

Old bankers boxes sat on the floor in a corner of his office, dusty, looking like cold-case files, waiting for Sherlock Holmes, Matlock or Perry Mason to come to their rescue, while District Attorney Tom Hardy sat pecking away at the keyboard of his computer.

He was very serious about his job. A graduate of Yale Law School— he was the most feared district attorney in all of Clark county, whenever he took a case, there was personal interest, and he didn't take the case of the ex-metro officer until Criminal Defense Attorney Summer Sinclair volunteered to represent him in court. When asked by a reporter why he jumped on the case, he responded by saying it was in the best interest of justice. Only he knew what he meant by that.

He finished his typing and sat slumped in his chair, wondering if he had time to personally go look at the scene to possibly create more doubt that things couldn't have went the way Mr. Gaines had claimed. He peered down at his wrist to check the time. *Not today* he thought.

He slid his chair back from underneath his desk and scooped his jacket from off the back of the chair and draped it over his shoulder, then headed for the door, he'd promised one of his colleagues that he would attend her ten-year-old daughter's birthday party. He had just enough time to shower and change his clothes, nearly everyone from the office was supposed to be there.

CHAPTER 28

Kerry backed out of her driveway, looking in both directions. She was terrified after hearing about the mysterious burgundy Toyota still lurking around the area where her family was supposed to feel safe, but she couldn't show her intimidation in front of her daughter or Heather.

She peered into her rearview mirror and saw them being friendly with each other the way they always were while sitting in the backseat of her Path-finder.

She hit the corner of Beech Family Street and made a right hand turn on Craig road. As soon as she got into traffic, she had to hold her breath when she spotted the flashing lights of a Highway Patrol SUV. It had a burgundy Toyota pulled over and detained—the driver of the car was standing in front of the patrol car with his legs spread, arms raised with his fingers clasped together in back of his head. She gasped, wondering if it was the same vehicle that had been chronically bothering her family, then she realized that the car she was staring at was a convertible, unlike the one she'd seen on the morning that she was taking care of her garden. She was relieved as she glanced at the girls through the rearview mirror to make sure they hadn't seen her discomfort. She was satisfied they hadn't.

She calmed down and switched on the car's radio and proceeded toward Alexander Shaw High School. She had a few errands to run once she dropped them off, and if things went according to plan, she would return home around the same time as her husband who had an appointment with his lawyer to work on his defense.

The scent of freshly brewed coffee filled the air at the Law Offices of Summer Sinclair. She sat at her desk, black hair pinned up and shining, smelling sweet like a fruit of sorts, wearing mid-height expensive red bottomed heels, sheer stockings, and a tight black knee-length skirt. Her form-fitting blouse couldn't hide the erection of her nipples—the impression they made could not be ignored.

Her client Kevin Gaines sat across the desk from her, trying his hardest to focus on the stack of papers sitting before him. She explained to him that it was only a portion of the discovery of the case that the State of Nevada was building against him, and that it would grow larger in volume as the case progressed. She also expressed that the evidence they had was largely circumstantial, but there were many sitting in prison who were convicted of less.

He stared at her plump well-shaped breasts and the hard nipples that protruded through her blouse, and found it extremely difficult to focus on anything she was saying to him.

She caught his gaze and immediately stood up and walked over to her copy machine, knowing damn well she didn't have anything that she wanted to copy, but it would give him an opportunity to make his move. She saw him turn through her peripheral as she neared the copier. As soon as she reached the hi-tech machine, she felt the firm masculine body of her lover press against her body from the back. He kissed the right side of her neck as his hand squeezed and rubbed her ass aggressively. She reached back and grabbed a hold of his erect penis. She then unzipped his loose-fitting slacks and freed his large member through the peehole and began massaging it with her soft and skillful hand. He knew that she wanted him inside her mouth, but it would have to wait, his craving was to plow deep inside her repeatedly.

He used both of his hands to raise her skirt. He settled it comfortably around her petite waist and looked down at her smooth well-shaped ass, her cotton pink panties were fitted snugly in its crevice. He peeled them out, slowly, and was tempted to drop down to his knees on the floor behind her to dine at her body's buffet—some creamy white cakes, a prime fresh pretty-pink asshole, a beautifully shaved vagina, and some nice delicate thighs were the only things on the menu. He had an appetite for all of it, but knew they didn't have much time, so he held her from behind and nudged her to bend over. She obliged, and when she did, she spread open her selection of goodies and allowed him to choose. He chose her delicious moist vagina. He guided his erection to its opening and pushed slowly and gently into it and felt himself sinking into what felt like heaven, and continued to push forward until he was balls deep.

She received his twelve-inch endowment, greedily, and with ease, thrusting her hips backward, grinding into him, trying to take him even deeper inside of her—she'd been longing for his thick dick to fill up her pussy, no other man made her feel fulfilled the way he did. She wished he had time to ram it up her ass the way she liked it, but she knew she wouldn't be able to conceal her cries. His dick felt so good inside of her. It scratched her walls, gave her a workout, quenched her sexual appetite and her need to feel desired, all in one feat. She was in love with her best friend's husband, and with him, she loved being fucked like a slut, and loved even more how it allowed her to live her personal life since her professional life made her feel so limited.

They both tried to keep their voices down as they reached climax. He ejaculated inside of her as she orgasmed all over his rod—she reached for some rags that were intended for the cleaning of the copy machine—she used them to clean them both up.

She hoped for a second round later on that evening, but the morning fuck was more than sufficient—they parted ways smiling as always...

CHAPTER 29

The in-chambers meeting with Judge Mitchell Fields, Criminal Defense Attorney Summer Sinclair, her investigator Gerald Osby, and District Attorney Randolph Stevens—a stand-in for Tom Hardy, was spontaneous and awfully uncomfortable.

Summer knew that her investigator, being a black man himself, understood a lot more than she ever would about what it's like to be a person of color in the United States of America, and how unfairly the legal system treated people of color, so she allowed him to speak freely about what he thought.

"Your Honor. Mr. Stevens. I have a lot of respect for both of you, but it's cases like these that makes me frown at this system that you call justice," he said before continuing. "Forgive me for not perceiving it the way you do. To me, it's more injustice than justice, especially when it comes to people with a tinted complexion, whether it be black, brown, Asian or something in-between, it's almost certain they won't receive justice—it seems to only be preserved for white people," he said articulately.

"Sir, I'm sorry you feel that way," said Judge Fields while glancing at District Attorney Stevens to see his reaction, then he looked at Summer and caught her looking at him. "Mr. Osby, I was under the impression that everyone here was a professional, but I now see how wrong I was."

"Your Honor, please, let's not be disrespectful," Summer interjected. "I'm in the business of practicing law. I take great pride in my firm and my accomplishments, and I consider myself as being very professional, therefore, anyone who works for me is professional as well," she told him. "Don't jump down my investigator's throat because he voiced his opinion—this is America where freedom of speech is provided as one of our rights, am I right?"

District Attorney Randolph Stevens was known in his office for being a liberal. He was probably as rational as they come when it came to district attorneys, he was known as Mr. Softy around his office.

"There's no need for anyone to get upset," he said calmly. "This meeting was strictly off the record, and I'm just filling in for my boss who couldn't be here. However, it's not uncommon for a defense lawyer to meet privately with a judge or a district attorney in an attempt to reach a compromise for their client, but I've never ever witnessed or been a part of any meeting, whether it be in a judge's chamber, my office, a café, or an elevator for that matter, where an attorney was outshined by their investigator."

"I'm here because my boss asked me to be," said Mr. Osby. "I just happen to be the one doing all of the digging on the case your office is trying to build against Kevin Gaines. In my opinion, thus far, everything that's been unearthed is in favor of the defense. That's why Mrs. Sinclair has requested that the case be dismissed, or for the charge to be reduced, at least, or that a better deal be offered to Mr. Gaines."

"All of your requests have been denied," said Judge Fields. "D.A. Stevens as well as Mr. Hardy, believe the state has a fair chance of getting a conviction in this case, and I'm inclined to believe them until a jury declares otherwise. Mr. Gaines will have to wait to see what a jury decides—I have every intention of moving forward."

Summer uncrossed her legs then crossed them again. She was unsure as to whether or not she should voice her opinion, but to prevent herself from doing further damage, she decided to stay quiet.

"Judge, what's happening in this case is a disservice to everyone and it undermines everything that our civil rights leaders marched and stood up for in this country," Mr. Osby stated. "There is no evidence whatsoever to try Kevin Gaines for second-degree murder. You know that but you refuse to dismiss this wobbly-fabricated case you have against him."

"Mr. Osby, if you're so sure about that, let the State of Nevada present its case to a jury and let that jury decide. That's how this process works. It has nothing to do with civil rights, its leaders, or any of that crap," replied Judge Fields.

"That's a slap in the face of public opinion," the investigator replied. "This process defeats the purpose of every civil rights activist/advocate that ever lived—Marcus Garvey, Medgar Evers, Martin Luther King Junior, and countless others. Black people as a whole still haven't reached the mountain-top Martin Luther King Junior talked about in his famous I Have A Dream speech. And as long as people like you exist, I personally don't see us ever reaching that mountaintop."

"Enough, Gerald! That's enough!" insisted Mrs. Sinclair. "My god, what's wrong with you? What are you doing?"

"I'm sorry, boss," Mr. Osby said. "I got carried away."

"You're out of line, way out of line," she continued. "You're not help-ing Mr. Gaines with this kind of rhetoric. You're hurting him more than you're helping him."

"I'm sorry if I offended anyone, and please, don't punish Mr. Gaines for my ignorance. I apologize sincerely to all of you," he said, humbly.

"Gerald, I really think you should take the rest of the day off. We'll talk about this later," his boss told him.

He just looked at Summer and shook his head. He backed toward the door with his face filled with shame, pulled it open and whispered 'I'm sorry' once more before leaving.

The air inside the chamber shifted as soon as he made his departure.

The remaining three were clueless as to what they should say.

"Mr. Stevens, I need a moment with Mrs. Sinclair, would you mind excusing yourself?" asked Judge Fields, trying to suppress his anger.

"Not at all," said Mr. Stevens as he stood up. "It's been interesting. You two have a wonderful day—I'll be in touch. I'll explain to Mr.Hardy how things went."

"Likewise," Judge Fields told him.

Summer smiled at him and gave him a nod.

As soon as District Attorney Stevens made his exit, Judge Fields turned to look at the defense attorney, and began speaking in a serious tone. "Who is this racist bastard you brought in here with you?"

She had a feeling this sort of tongue-lashing was coming, and although she was upset herself, she was prepared to do all she could to stand up for her investigator—she wished the police department had done the same for Lieutenant Gaines. She uncrossed her legs and stood up.

"Your Honor, with all due respect, neither you or I know from personal experience what it feels like to be a black man in this country. My investigator and my client have that in common. He's investigating a case where a then, black male lieutenant, only because he was in fear of his life, rightfully and justifiably shot and killed a person who happened to be white while in the line of duty, and because the victim was white and unarmed, they've stripped the once-lieutenant of his job, ruining any chance of him ever having a successful career in law enforcement, even if he is acquitted of the charge. None of this would be happening if the roles were reversed—I dare you to disagree," she said.

The judge looked at her as if he couldn't believe his ears. He began to wonder if the words spoken by her investigator were really his or hers—she seemed to have the same viewpoint in common that her employee expressed—it angered him to think she'd put him up to it. "Mrs. Sinclair, are you sure that's the path you wish to embark?"

"I am," she said with confidence.

"…Then, be careful."

She paused, but kept her poise. "Is that a threat, judge?"

"No…it's a warning!" he said sternly.

She was puzzled. "Should I be afraid?"

"That's your decision—I'm just telling you that a different path would be your best bet."

She was really frightened at that point. The reiterated threat was now imminent. "I don't like the sound of this," she told him.

"Neither would I," he said, displaying tyranny.

She left his chamber. Nervous. She wasn't quite sure what he was saying to her, but she was certain that it violated ethics. She had no idea what she'd gotten herself into, and she found herself hoping she'd get out of it safely. It was a side of the legal system that she was unfamiliar with—the danger she sensed made her tremble inside.

Just outside the front door of Judge Fields' courtroom, she accidentally bumped into a woman who was walking past, looking down at the phone she held in her hand, neither was paying attention to what they were doing. "Oh, I'm sorry, Caitlyn," she said apologetically, immediately recognizing the attorney who once worked for her.

"Geez, Summer, how could you not see me as big as I am?" she said smiling.

"I'm sorry," Summer said again. "I don't know where my mind is, lately it's been all over the place."

"Are you okay?" asked Caitlyn.

"I'm fine, just tired I guess?" she lied, still rattled by the threat Judge Fields had made.

"Are you sure, you don't seem like yourself?" she asked, examining her closely.

"I'm sure. I'm okay."

"How's Heather and Matt?"

"Everyone's fine, how about your family?"

"Every day is a struggle, but we're making it work," Caitlyn said casually. "You made things look so easy when I worked for you; I didn't realize running a law office would be so hard."

Summer smiled. Her extracurricular activities behind the scenes is what kept her office afloat, but, of course, Caitlyn was too square to know that. Rules sometimes had to be bent in order to get ahead in the legal field, but since Caitlyn followed the law to the letter, struggling would more than likely continue to be part of her journey. Summer was hesitant, but she decided to speak to Caitlyn indirectly, it would be up to her to catch on.

"Caitlyn, you can't wait for life to yield you a break, sometimes you just have to make your own, and it may require you to bend a little," she said sincerely.

"Things'll get better, they'll work out. They have to," said Caitlyn.

"I hope so," said Summer. "Let me get out of here, I'll talk to you later."

"Have a great day—as they say, break a leg."

"You too, Caitlyn," Summer said smiling.

CHAPTER 30

For Kevin Gaines, it seemed everything that reminded him of his unusual predicament came rumbling back first thing in the morning. He wanted nothing more than to go running to a nearby dispensary, since weed was legal, and get some kind of cush that would effortlessly keep negative thoughts at bay, but he needed something more permanent than the temporary fix. He needed his problem to go away completely.

His attorney sat beside him as he and his wife lay in bed, trying her best to convince him to see things her way. She was very uncomfortable with the way things were, especially after being threatened by the presiding judge. Yes, she was defiant. Determined. Focused. Success-driven. Combative, and was more confident than anyone she knew, but at the end of the day, when all things were said and spoken for, and her career was over, she wanted to still be alive. She was a loving mom, a wife, a companion, a lover, a best friend, and she didn't want any aspect of it being jeopardized.

She wanted her and Matt to grow old together, although she felt he deserved someone better than her. She wanted to be by Heather's side, supporting her 110% when she went to college and attended medical school, and was certified as a registered nurse. She wasn't prepared to say goodbye to her daughter's aspirations, but this case alone could ruin it all, she thought. She kept taking glances at Kerry as she talked to Kevin, whom was rubbing his head while listening to her.

"Kevin, I was under the impression that Internal Affairs or the Metropolitan Police Department, Chief Dunlap in particular, or possibly Mayor Kason, to have pushed for this case to be filed against you, but after I was literally threatened yesterday by a judge to be careful and told to think about my family, I don't know if it's best to withdraw myself from this case, or try to convince you that it would probably be in your best interest to take a plea bargain?"

Kevin's head kept nodding as he struggled to accept what she'd said—his mind shifted back to Juanita Howard, the attorney from the police union. *Why is everyone trying to convince me to take a deal* he wondered.

"Baby, you should probably listen to her. I'm scared too," Kerry pleaded.

"Baby, I can't volunteer to leave you and Ke'Auna. What happens to y'all if they send me to prison?"

"What about Matt and Heather if I stay on this thing?" Summer interjected. "This case doesn't make sense to me. It scares me."

"…It doesn't make sense to me either," Kevin finally said. "It's like trying to make sense out of an eagle swooping down from the sky just to catch a fly. I have no idea why this case was filed against me, and why everyone suddenly turned on me? Does this happen in everyone's life, or is it just my black life, I don't get it?"

Summer caught the strong gaze that was coming from Kerry. She tilted her head, frowned, and slumped her shoulders—she knew what the unrelenting stare signified, or was it something else? "…Kevin, I promised your wife and daughter that I would get you out of this mess. I'm frightened but I'm going to keep my word," she said.

"Thank you," he said. "Now what?"

"Like I said, I thought Internal Affairs or metro had pushed this case into the limelight by filing charges against you. I found out yesterday who's really behind it."

"Who is it?" asked Kevin, beating Kerry to the punch.

"A hard-nosed D.A. by the name of Tom Hardy. He's the Deputy D.A. and a tough cookie from what I hear," Summer told him. "I'll try to talk to him soon and see if I can feel him out. I've never had to go to him directly before, but I know for a fact he can drop this thing. He may be the only one who can," she said with emphasis.

"Well, keep us posted," said Kevin.

"I won't let them win, Kevin," Summer said with confidence as she got off the edge of the bed and stood awkwardly beside it. "Let me see if I can work my magic. I'll be in touch."

Kevin and Kerry both nodded their heads.

Summer made her exit and hit the trail. Her first thought was to have her investigator Gerald Osby do some probing—she sent him a text, then her mind switched to the dinner she knew her husband had planned for her later that evening—something she really looked forward to, a nice meal and some hot, kinky dessert would really do her body some good—but since she still had the entire day ahead of her, she might as well see what she could make of it, she thought.

She went downtown to the District Attorney's Office, and lo and behold, she came face to face with Mr. Tom Hardy. He was reluctant to sit down with her at first, but after a few minutes of convincing, he agreed to give her five minutes of his time, no deal was reached, but he did give her something to cogitate…

Later that evening, she and her husband were enjoying an exquisite meal of crab legs and hot-melted butter, tobasco sauce, and an expensive bottle of champagne that was slightly chilled but still on ice.

Summer pranced around the dining room, wearing a see-through pair of red-laced panties, jutting her ass upward, then into her husband's face as he sat at the dining room table, pulling her panties aside as he worked his tongue, performing analingus on her. He momentarily pulled his face away from her buttocks to reinflate his lungs as she forced herself backward while he ate her groceries.

"Ooooh, yessss, Matt. That's it!" she said in a breathy somewhat raspy voice. She used one hand to grab the back of a chair, the other latched onto her crotch as she began rubbing her labia and clitoris aggressively through the thin fabric of her delicates as her husband's tongue penetrated her anus—she found herself convulsing with her eyes closed.

Her energy was depleted when she finished coming. On a scale of one to ten, she gave Matt a six when it came to intercourse, but boy, she loved his tongue. She gave that a ten, she couldn't have imagined such an orgasm.

For some reason, her mind took her back to earlier in the day when she sat down with Deputy District Attorney Tom Hardy. He wouldn't budge when it came to rethinking the case against her client Kevin Gaines, but he made a statement she was certain to never forget. He told her, *"Everything about this system is corrupt. Everybody as well…and, when I say everybody, I mean everybody…."*

Why would he make such a statement? She really needed to find out, and the sooner the better, she thought to herself.

CHAPTER 31

Summer woke up the next morning with more energy than she knew what to do with. She heard Matt when he'd gotten up to get dressed for work, but she stayed in bed until he left. She did a quick workout before taking a shower. It wasn't her full routine; she skipped the stretching, and did ten sets apiece of squats and crunches—repetitions varied with each set.

She didn't have to be in court until 1:30 that afternoon, where one of her clients was scheduled to have an evidentiary hearing in front of a judge that was new to the bench. She had no idea how it would turn out.

She gave Kerry a call and invited her to a massage at a brand new massage parlor called Sequoya's—not far from the Strip. It was its grand opening and she wanted them to be there for the ribbon-cutting ceremony—they were offering free massages to the first one-hundred customers, the advertisements she'd seen made it look upscale and classy, and there would also be complimentary champagne and strawberries, something she nor Kerry could ever get enough of.

She figured since Kerry was an early bird she'd be up to it, and it would be a great way for them to relieve some stress, something she was certain they both needed.

It turned out to be a wonderful time. They enjoyed their massages, especially while under the influence of champagne. Summer still had to go to work that afternoon, so she was hoping she hadn't over consumed.

"It feels like a ton of bricks have been lifted from my shoulders," Kerry said as she climbed in the passenger side and pulled the door shut.

"I feel the same way. That was great," Summer said as she backed out of the parking space, looking in both directions. "We have to do this again someday."

"Absolutely. The sooner the better," Kerry agreed. "I feel good for real, like my world done been rocked!"

Both women laughed. They spoke briefly about the case on their drive back home, but mostly about the wonderful experience they had at Sequoya's—they vowed to do it again soon.

The car came bursting around the corner just to run into two Highway Patrol cruisers that were sitting there waiting for it. They got a call from another patrol unit a couple of minutes earlier about a car that was speeding and ignoring commands to stop—they knew it was headed straight to them.

"Driver, get out slowly and place your hands in the air!" one of the Troopers said. "Get out slowly, don't try anything."

The door of the burgundy two-door Toyota Lexus flew open as the driver purposely got out. A small figure, in full compliance, held their hands straight up in the air and moved from the space between the car and door.

"Stop where you are! Keep your hands up where I can see them!" the Trooper yelled.

"Please, don't shoot. I'm doing everything you're telling me to," a woman was heard saying, clearly terrified.

"Ma'am, what are you doing? What were you thinking, and why didn't you pull over and stop when we asked you to?"

"Scared I guess. I don't know."

"You don't know?"

"I was scared, officer. I wasn't exactly expecting to run into trouble."

"That's an understatement."

"Tell me about it," the woman stated as she placed her hands behind her back, allowing her wrists to be cuffed. Ten minutes later, a tow truck showed up and towed her vehicle.

She was taken into custody without incident, and after reaching the station, it didn't take much to find out that she was Amy Forbes—the mother of Shane Forbes—it only took seconds to determine after running her fingerprints, she had no identification in her possession.

She also confessed that it was in fact her burgundy Toyota Lexus that had been circling the Oceanblue Estates as well as Alexander Shaw High School.

During her interrogation, she admitted that she'd in fact attempted to kidnap Ke'Auna, and added, "I wanted him to experience firsthand what it felt like to lose a child. To have something so near and dear ripped from your life forever, and not be able to do anything to stop it."

The officer searched the computer and couldn't find any report relating to any abduction attempt, he began to think she was lying to him until he saw her reaction when he told her there was no record of it. "Wait a minute and let me contact the chief," he told her.

It was nearly ten minutes when he returned, but he had some news for her that shocked them both. "Well, Amy, this is your lucky day," he said without sitting down. "There's no record of the attempted kidnapping that you volunteered to tell me, therefore, I can't use it against you."

"Awesome," she said immediately.

"Also, I talked to the chief and explained the situation to him, and he instructed me to just ticket you for the few traffic violations and let you go. If it's true that you attempted to kidnap that officer's daughter, and failed, be thankful not ungrateful. You failing is why that young girl is safe and with her parents, and also why you're able to walk out of here today."

Amy thought the officer made a good point. "You're right," she said. "I feel like God is giving me a second chance."

"That's a good way to look at it," the officer told her. "Out of curiosity, how did you become aware of the officer's daughter and where she goes to school?"

"…Uh…the internet," she said as if she thought he should have already known.

Fortunately for her, since she hadn't been caught in the act, it was decided that she was a grieving, heartbroken mother who had already been through enough.

Having to pay traffic tickets turned out to be a blessing. She gave a sigh and looked at it as a learning experience. Lord knows it could have been worse, she thought.

She was entirely relieved when she left the jail. The experience gave her a new lease on life.

CHAPTER 32

Things became topsy-turvy for the two families. Summer had already promised to stay on the case, but after death threats against her family continued, she was once again threatening to abandon her post.

It had been a week since they learned Amy Forbes was the sole perpetrator behind the attempted abduction of Ke'Auna Gaines, and even after giving a voluntary statement of what happened, since the officers who answered the call on the night in question failed to file a report, no charges could be filed against the perp.

Summer thought it was amiss that no one had stepped forward or offered to look into the numerous threats made against her and her family, of which she thought was absurd, but she sensed the threats would immediately cease if she pulled off the case. Kevin nor Kerry understood her point, and because of that, all of their relationships became strained.

It can't be said with absolute certainty, but whoever said *a family that prays together stays together* is wrong, but at the very least, it's questionable. The Sinclairs and Gaines were like one big family, before the case began, they'd often attended church services together or came together just to pray, but the case at hand, jeopardized it all.

"This is ridiculous, Summer. We've already covered this topic, and you gave my family your word that you would stay on the case. Why are we discussing it again now?" Kerry asked in frustration.

Summer looked at her friend of whom she knew was hurting inside, but still, she didn't have an easy answer for her. She actually thought of Kevin, and as inappropriate as it was, she wished he was available and could scratch the uncontrollable itch she felt between her legs, but she knew that her timing couldn't have been more wrong.

"I'm just concerned for my family. That's all," she said. "The courts have been ruling against me constantly and I'm not used to that. Law enforcement isn't taking these death threats seriously, and it's all starting to bother me like you wouldn't believe."

She continued, "I need to take a break and get away from it all. At least for awhile."

"Who are you fooling, Summer? C'mon girl. A break? We both know that aint happening—the best thing to do is face it head on," Kerry told her.

"Easy to say for someone whose family and livelihood isn't in jeopardy."

"Bitch, we must not be on the same planet?" said Kerry, not able to control her anger. "If these crooked motherfuckers convict my husband for a crime even they know he didn't commit, he'll go to prison, and that leaves me and Ke'Auna where? Don't tell me my family isn't in jeopardy. Been there and done that—you know that."

Summer paused. She gave a sigh as if she'd temporarily forgotten that both families were at risk, then reached out and placed her hand on Kerry's forearm. "You're right. I'm sorry. I've got so much on my mind that I can't even think straight. Give me a little time and I'll figure it out."

"We all need to just take a step back to refresh our minds. Everything will be fine if we hold on to our faith," Kerry said in a consoling voice.

"I agree," said Summer. She left the Gaines' residence heading to her downtown office—she sent her investigator a text to see if he'd learned anything new.

Private Investigator Gerald Osby was a little over the top where the lines were drawn between black and white, but he loved his job and was good at it. He was thorough in everything he did, where investigating was concerned, and if it hadn't been for his extreme nature to be thorough—acting on hunches and intuition—he probably wouldn't have returned to the corner of Rainbow and Warm Springs for the umpteenth time since his boss had taken on the challenge to defend the officer who was accused of deliberately pulling the trigger and murdering unarmed nineteen-year-old Shane Forbes.

One thing he knew about life was that it was unpredictable. The strangest things could happen at any time, and on this day, the unpredictable happened.

He entered the Starbucks next door to the Moneytree store that Shane Forbes was acting erratically in the morning he was killed, and without warning, ran into Sasha Caldwell, one of his old acquaintances, who he learned had a connection to someone involved in the case he was currently working on. The information he gathered was priceless. He immediately went into overdrive trying to get confirmation to what he'd learned. He ended up visiting the underworld to get his answers. It only took him a few stops to connect the dots, he immediately sent his boss a text message requesting a meeting—he was more anxious than ever to expose his discovery.

CHAPTER 33

Humidity in the air was thick as the massive cloud-cover made it appear to be evening instead of the early morning.

Investigator Gerald Osby swung his car into a handicap parking spot directly in front of police headquarters, and then looked around casually as he made his exit. He had no plans to stay inside for long, so he hoped he wouldn't be ticketed for the illegal parking. He worked for a lawyer for Christ's sake, and knew he shouldn't be breaking the law, but he didn't feel like being sweaty and sticky from being outside longer than necessary, so the closer he parked to the entrance, the sooner he could get inside and away from the unpleasant elements.

The walking distance to reach the entrance from the parking lot wasn't all that long, but every step saved outdoors made a huge difference in monsoon season—more than likely, the humidity would only get worse as the day progressed, he thought.

It was 9:58 when he pushed through the doors—the pre-arranged meeting was to start at 10:00. It seemed more people than he was aware of was expecting his arrival, because as soon as he stopped to look for direction, a janitor who appeared to be cleaning up a spill, pointed him toward Chief Dunlap's office—he gave the janitor a thumbs up as he headed towards it.

He used the back of his hand and knocked once, then turned the door-knob and entered without waiting to be invited inside. He felt the important meeting should have happened the night before when he expressed its urgency, and that he'd already waited longer than he should have—he wasn't prepared to wait any longer.

Two men were inside the office just as he expected, and Chief Dunlap stopped talking in mid-sentence and looked at him like he was out of line for entering his office. "Good morning, gentlemen," he said as he closed the door behind him, then rushed over to shake both sets of hands.

"Howdy," Chief Dunlap replied. "You must be Mr. Osby?"

"I am, and you must be the chief?" he said, joking. He'd seen both men on television on more than one occasion, so he was very aware of them. There was no reason before the present for either of the two men to be aware of him.

"Yes. I thought that maybe the uniform might speak for itself? This here is Mayor Kason, in case you haven't met?"

"Mayor, it's a pleasure," he said respectfully. "We've never met, but, naturally, I know who you are—and even if I didn't, there's an aura about you that exudes power."

"Thank you, Mr. Osby," the mayor said, smiling. "I really wasn't expecting a compliment so early in the day, but one like that is always welcome. I was told by the chief that you had information you wanted to discuss with me personally, otherwise, I probably wouldn't be here," he said, his smile completely dissipated.

"Well, mayor, I'm pleased that you were able to make it. Thank you, and yes, I do have something I want to discuss with you. I'd rather talk to you about it first, in hopes that we won't have to involve the press," he said. He knew what kind of power the two men possessed, but what he'd unearthed the day before was so damaging, he felt it gave him the upper hand, they'd want more than anything to keep him quiet. "You know they're always interested in a juicy story, especially the ones that are downright sinister."

Mayor Kason shifted uncomfortably in his seat, then reached over and poured himself a glass of water. "Well, what is it—beating around the bush isn't going to get us to it?" he said after taking a sip.

"I need one of you gentlemen to please explain to me why charges were filed against Kevin Gaines?"

"A crime was committed," spat Chief Dunlap, not giving the mayor a chance to respond.

"Chief, do you really believe that, or were you ordered by someone else to press charges?"

Chief Dunlap glanced at Mayor Kason, hoping he'd intervene, but he didn't. He didn't appreciate the tone of the investigator's voice, or where the line of questioning was going—personally, he never wanted to press charges against his ex-lieutenant, but he was urged relentlessly to do so.

He felt like a fish that was struggling to breathe as he flopped back and forth outside of his tank. Chief Dunlap felt completely cornered, so he answered the question reluctantly. "I believe he committed murder. The young man he killed was unarmed and never posed a threat."

"I'm sorry chief, were you there that day?" asked Mr. Osby.

"No, I wasn't."

"So how can you say a threat was never posed?"

"The deceased was a kid and was unarmed," Mayor Kason interjected.

"Just because he was young doesn't mean he couldn't be a threat. You know that," said the investigator. "You must have been there, mayor—were you there?"

Mayor Kason swallowed hard before speaking. "Neither of us were there, but a thorough investigation was done, and we have faith in the reports of our investigators," he said. He didn't like being put on the hot seat, especially by someone he felt was beneath him.

Mr. Osby turned to Chief Dunlap. He stared into his eyes before he spoke. "Sir, how long was Kevin Gaines employed by Metro?"

"I believe it was somewhere around twenty-five years."

"Twenty-five long years?'

"Yes," said the chief.

"That's a long time," Mr. Osby stated. "Wouldn't you agree?"

"I would. It's a very long time," said the chief.

"Was Mr. Gaines a loyal employee?"

"Yes. Very."

"Any complaints against him from the public or his colleagues?"

"None that I know of," replied the chief.

"Did you like Mr. Gaines, chief?"

"Absolutely."

"You two got along pretty good?"

"Absolutely."

"Did you trust him?"

"With my life," the chief answered immediately.

"You trusted him with your life?"

"I most certainly did. Probably still would," Chief Dunlap admitted.

"When you talked to him about that fateful morning, did he tell you he felt his life was threatened?"

"He told me that. Yes."

"So what happened, did you not believe him?"

"I believed him," the chief admitted. "I never said I didn't believe him."

The investigator paused after detecting the contradiction. He didn't want Chief Dunlap to become too uncomfortable. After all, he was the one who had made the meeting possible, so he didn't want to punish or ridicule him by turning the meeting into an interrogation, especially since Chief Dunlap wasn't his target. "So, you did believe him when he told you Shane Forbes had threatened his safety, even though you stated a few moments ago that no threat was posed? We won't delve into that, chief. I'm ready to leave that alone, because I believe you when you stated you believed Mr. Gaines."

"He's a good man," the chief added.

"You and I both know that," Mr. Osby told him.

Chief Dunlap breathed a sigh of relief. He felt the weight of the world had been lifted from his shoulders; he'd gotten so tired of carrying it around.

Mr. Osby turned his attention to Mayor Kason. "Are you responsible for the charges, sir?"

"You really have some nerves, Mr. Investigator," Mayor Kason stated, his anger apparent, but he saw that Gerald Osby wasn't backing down.

"Is that a yes or no?"

"I instructed the chief to press charges, yes," the mayor answered.

Mr. Osby shook his head. He thought of all the turmoil Kevin Gaines and his family had been through, now he was standing face to face with the man who was behind it all. "Why?"

"He committed murder," the mayor replied. "What he did was un-called for."

"Mr. Mayor, with all due respect, we've already established that you weren't there so you have no right to say what was or wasn't called for," the investigator told him.

Chief Dunlap watched and listened, praying silently that he wouldn't be asked anymore questions.

"Again, everything was thoroughly investigated. My knowledge is based solely on the reports I've read and the verbal accounts I received."

"Mayor, let me tell you why I don't believe you," Mr. Osby said, candidly. "Even with the reports from your so called investigators, you spoke to Chief Dunlap here I'm sure, and I'm more than certain that what he's told you contradicts any report you've read, am I right?"

Mayor Kason was afraid to answer the question. He began to wonder if he needed his lawyer. "Chief Dunlap was hesitant at first, but I understand," he began. "It's quite difficult to bring yourself to press charges against one of your own, especially one as serious as this."

"But you kept insisting?"

"I might have, yes," said the mayor.

Investigator Osby once again averted his attention. "Chief, did you feel pressured, as if you had no choice but to charge Mr. Gaines for the murder of Shane Forbes?"

Chief Dunlap nodded slowly before replying, "Yes."

"Well, Mayor Kason, we know you pressured the chief into bringing charges against Mr. Gaines, were there any outside influences pressing you?"

"Of course not," the mayor told him.

"Are you sure?"

"I believe I've already answered that, Mr. Investigator. Excuse me if I don't understand your question."

"You don't, huh?" the investigator said.

"Mr. Osby are you implying something?" the mayor asked, suspicious.

The investigator stared into his eyes and said, "Should I be?" Before the mayor could give a reply, the investigator turned away from him and looked at Chief Dunlap, whose face had suddenly turned a bright red. Immediately, he began to feel bad, because the expression he saw made it clear to him that the man must have thought that he was in some kind of trouble. "Chief, why did he say it was so important to charge Mr. Gaines?"

Chief Dunlap paused as he turned to his boss. He was done being intimidated. He answered the question, looking directly into his pupils, "He said we had to appease the public, and that he and I would be out of our jobs if we sat back and did nothing."

"Out of your jobs?" Mr. Osby repeated. "Oh, he wanted to make it seem like your future was at stake?"

"That's what he said," said Chief Dunlap.

"Mayor, this is a bad spot for you, isn't it?" the investigator asked. "Losing your jobs had nothing to do with it, neither did pleasing the public."

"Public opinion means everything in politics," the mayor said.

"I don't disagree with that, mayor, but it had nothing to do with this," the investigator told him. "This isn't just rhetoric, and I don't make it a habit to speak on things that aren't true, so I welcome you to step in if what I'm saying is false."

Mayor Kason didn't say anything.

"Mayor, who pressed you to shit on the chief so he could shit on Mr. Gaines?"

Again, no word from Mayor Kason, but the anger he felt was imminent.

"Let me ask you this then, Mr. Mayor," began Mr. Osby. "Is it true that you know Amy Forbes personally? In fact, you two have history so to speak, am I correct?"

"I know her, but I wouldn't say we have history," the mayor said nervously, looking at the chief for a reaction.

"No history?" asked the investigator. "You were one of her regulars before she retired from her profession, and you know damn well what profession I'm referring to. If that's not history, what would you call it?"

Silence from Mayor Kason, but this time, his silence spoke volumes.

"This isn't court, but don't answer that, mayor. I wouldn't want you to incriminate yourself, and you don't need your lawyers, at least not yet," Mr. Osby told him. "That's also why no charges were brought against Amy, am I right? Sorry, don't answer that either. Get rid of this ridiculous case against Kevin Gaines and all of this goes away. No one will ever have to know about your past," he continued. "Our office hope to hear soon that the case was dropped against Mr. Gaines. I'm sure you and the chief have something to talk about, so I'll leave you to it, but we'll be expecting a word from you soon."

The investigator returned to his car, and was relieved to see that he had no ticket. The humidity in the air was still thick, but he felt good. He believed the life of Kevin Gaines was about to get better. He had no idea how wrong he was.

CHAPTER 34

"Oooh, giirrlll, look at you. Are you sure your mom will approve of you lookin' so sexy?" Ke'Auna laughed as she viewed Heather from behind as they stood in front of the bathroom mirror.

Heather blushed as she brushed her long black hair; it spiraled in curls down the center of her back. "This is *nothing* in comparison to what she wears. She bought me this skirt, so she can't be mad."

"She didn't see it on you though, did she?"

Heather's smile widened. She had just been reminded of how well her friend knew her. "No, but it doesn't change the fact that she bought it for me."

"Great argument, but we'll see if it works," said Ke'Auna. "If a career in nursing doesn't work out for you, you probably should consider the legal field as an alternative?"

"Are you saying it could be in the genes?" laughed Heather.

"Could be."

"Are you jealous?" Heather asked. She pursed her lips.

"Maybe a little," Ke'Auna said playfully. "It would be cool if you became a lawyer, that means I'll have someone to borrow money from."

"You jerk," Heather said as she turned and playfully tapped her on the shoulder. "You're the one I was counting on to loan me money."

Both girls laughed as they exited the bathroom. They entered the living room where their parents were waiting.

As soon as Summer laid eyes on her daughter, her entire demeanor changed as she looked her up and down. "You look nice, sweetheart. You remind me of me when I was your age. Wow."

Heather glanced at Ke'Auna and smiled, then looked at her mom and said, "Thanks. Everyone knows you're gorgeous, so I take that as a compliment."

They were headed to the T-Mobile Arena to attend an NBA game—it was their first time frequenting the venue—The Los Angeles Lakers were hosting the San Antonio Spurs, but, of course, they were all Lakers fans.

They all assembled inside of Matthew's SUV, then the Ford Excursion shot up Beech Family Street like a dragster on a runway strip. Everyone was used to his fast driving, he drove everything like it was an ambulance in a hurry to some kind of emergency.

CHAPTER 35

Two days after their visit from Investigator Gerald Osby, Mayor Kason and Chief Dunlap were once again in each other's presence, dressed as sharp as a mosquito's needle, this time it was at the mayor's office, instead of police headquarters.

"Well, chief, this is the last thing I'll be requesting of you. Are you ready?" Mayor Kason said as he stood before him, straightening his tie.

"As ready as one can be."

"I appreciate you, chief. I really do," the mayor said as tears welled in his eyes. "I hope someday you'll forgive me for this."

Chief Scott Dunlap gave his superior a nod, then gestured with his hand for him to open up the door. "Let's get her done."

Mayor Kason pulled open the door and fell in behind the chief when he walked outside to the front lawn where camera crews were already set up and awaiting them. They were summoned by the mayor's personal assistant to be there, but all they knew was that there would be an announcement. They had no inkling of what it entailed.

Pictures instantly began snapping, several of them, back-to-back, as both men approached the podium that held a microphone.

Both men gave each other a long stare, then shook hands firmly before the mayor pulled the microphone from its holder and spoke directly into it. "Good afternoon to all of you," he began, looking from camera to camera. "Chief Dunlap and I are standing out here together in solidarity, because we have a very important announcement to make. Some of you will be grateful for it, and some of you will not. Nonetheless, it still has to be made, and once I announce it, we'll both be bound by it," he said before pausing.

"C'mon, mayor, let's hear it! Don't keep us in suspense," yelled one of the crewmembers. "Spit it out, please."

"Geez, I'm getting to it. Give me a chance," replied the mayor, issuing a grin. "I speak for myself and for Chief Dunlap. We've put a lot of thought into our decision, and once I announce it, it'll be final. I won't bother going into any of the details, nor will I be answering any questions, but for the interest of justice, Chief Dunlap and I hereby resign from our posts as the leaders of this city—effective immediately." He placed the microphone back in its holder, then turned in unison with Mr. Dunlap, and walked away from the podium—ducking back inside his office and shutting the door.

Everyone was shocked. Some ooohs and ahhhs were heard from some of the crewmembers. Some were still staring at each other with their mouths ajar as if they needed someone to pinch them to show them they weren't dreaming. Some were even left wondering if it was a joke, but it wasn't. The mayor of the great city of Las Vegas, as well as the Chief of Police, had just resigned simultaneously. No warning. No explanation. No two-week notice. It all happened live while the cameras were rolling—more than half of the general public was outraged.

Criminal Defense Lawyer Summer Sinclair and her investigator watched the announcement together in disbelief. You could hear a pin drop inside her office as they sat speechless, they could have never imagined receiving such a hit, but they both had an idea of what prompted it.

They're leverage to get the case dropped against their client had just vanished. They had no idea what to do next.

The criminal case against ex-lieutenant Kevin Gaines would continue. The people in his corner were devastated!

CHAPTER 36

Even with the huge *never forgetting distraction* of a pending trial, lingering; loitering; constantly hovering above them like a dark, frightening storm cloud, making everything seem gloomy, the Gaines' tried their best to live normally, even though they knew their future was uncertain.

The outcome of a trial could tear them apart forever if the verdict turns out to be an unfavorable one, and if that were to happen, what kind of future would Ke'Auna have, they wondered?

The past few days were terrible where the weather was concerned. For the most part, it was hot, humid, sticky and uncomfortable to the point where it was almost unbearable, so the majority of people chose to stay indoors unless it was absolutely imperative that they go outside. Every now and again the humidity would dissipate as well as the heat and leave in its trail a nice cool breeze that made it comfortable and ideal for most people, so instead of being cooped up indoors, it was seemingly a perfect time to get outside for those who needed to get their fix of fresh air—the Gaines' decided to take a stroll.

Back when everything was normal, it was commonplace to see Kevin and Kerry, and every now and then, Ke'Auna, walking or jogging up and down Beech Family Street and its surrounding streets to stay in shape. Unfortunately, since the murderer label had been placed on him, Kevin had been forced to stay indoors most of the time, not really in fear, but not knowing how safe he'd be if he drifted too far away from his home. It wasn't really himself that he was afraid for. His concern was for the safety of his wife and daughter, which was totally understandable to those who knew him. As far as he was concerned, his family was the sole reason he woke up each day—the very reason he breathed—every breath he took was for them— he just wanted them to be safe and taken care of.

He smiled as he jogged slowly behind Kerry, slowing down every time she did. He knew she wanted him to catch up and run beside her, but he was perfectly content with his position. It gave him a chance to admire her from afar—he was appreciative of the fact that the lack of exercise hadn't diminished her curves or anything else that contributed to her gorgeousness.

"Catch up, sweetie. Why are you hanging around back there?" she yelled when she turned around to look at him. She saw his smile broaden as she stared at him, so she stopped to see what was on his mind. "What's so funny?" she said, her intuition telling her what he was up to, she could also tell from the mannish smirk he had on his face that his mind was somewhere it had no business.

"Nothing," he said, smiling. "I'm just admiring my wife and all of her wonderful assets. It's a beautiful evening, and looking at you makes it even more beautiful."

"Awww. That's sweet, honey. Thank you," she said, wrapping her arms around him and giving him a peck on the lips.

"I love you," he said as he stared into her light brown eyes.

"Ditto," she said softly. "And it'll never change no matter what."

Hearing those words meant so much to him, he knew her love was genuine—it made him regret being unfaithful to her. *Lord, help me* he said to himself.

They walked the short distance to their home, side-by-side, arms wrapped around each other. When they made the turn to go up the driveway, he allowed her to go ahead of him again as they walked between the narrow space in-between his truck and the hedge bushes that lined the driveway. He found himself checking her out again. He loved how good she looked from the rear—her ample backside appeared to be swallowing the grey cotton sweatpants she wore. He'd never once seen a woman with an ass so perfect. Clearly mesmerized, he was still looking down at her bottom when she turned around to look at him—he just couldn't seem to help himself.

"Honey, why are you lookin' at my booty? You better stop being nasty," she said, smiling.

He reached down and grabbed a handful, palming one cheek as he squeezed firmly. He was turned on when he felt how warm and soft it was.

"Baby, your ass looks and feels so good; I don't know if I wanna eat it for dinner or save it for dessert," he said, grinning.

She blushed and covered her mouth with her hand, then let it fall to her side as they locked eyes. "You don't have to choose, sweetheart. It's all yours and you may do with it whatever you please. I think it's enough for dinner and dessert," she said as she placed her hand on his swollen genitals. "Oooh, it's already hard. You know baby, this booty can also serve as a bounce house, depending on whether or not you feel like jumping up and down in it?" she said sexily.

"Oooh, ooohhh! We gotta hurry up and get your ass in the house," he said as he nudged her forward, then hurried to close the gate behind them.

As soon as they entered the living room and the front door was safely secured, taking a shower was the farthest thing from their minds. They were eagerly at each other; kissing; licking; sucking; groping and speaking vulgarly—it wasn't long before articles of clothing began peeling and being torn off. Their goal was to get each other naked as quickly as possible, they didn't care that their clothes were strewn all over the place.

Their daughter was at the Sinclair residence hanging out with Heather. She wasn't expected to be home for a couple of hours, giving them plenty of time to get down and dirty, which was exactly what they did.

As expected, Ke'Auna came frolicking through the front door around 7:00 PM, hungry, and expecting dinner to be ready, but it wasn't. She entered the kitchen and saw her parents scrambling, and pulling stuff from the cabinets and freezer that was needed to prepare dinner, something that was normally already done. "I thought supper would be done already? I'm starving."

"It'll be ready soon, sweetie," her mom told her. "I got a late start. Sorry," she said sincerely.

Her dad said nothing. He was feeling guilty.

"I'll go ahead and take my shower first," Ke'Auna said. She knew what was up from the moment she entered the house and smelled the peculiar odor when she went through the living room, she recognized the scent of sex as soon as it hit her nostrils, she didn't know why her parents thought she was so naïve, she was truly a virgin but she wasn't stupid?

CHAPTER 37

Six months after the deadly shooting of nineteen-year-old Shane Forbes, the case files grew against the ex-lieutenant. Trial was set to take place in five days, and although the case built against him was mostly circumstantial, Deputy Prosecutor Tom Hardy wanted to be sure that all of the i's were dotted and the t's were crossed—he had no intention of making a fool of himself, losing for him, was not an option.

He sat erectly in the chair of his home office, thumbing through the Gaines' file one page at a time. He was still undecided about whether or not he would prepare a summation for closing arguments or just freestyle, he was good at both, so he wasn't worried.

He heard his part-time maid, Lindsay, as she neared his office and he looked up as soon as she appeared in the doorway.

"Would you like some tea, Mr. Hardy?" she said as she came in, wearing a tiny pair of white swim shorts and no panties underneath, a midriff white tank top and no bra, nor did she have on shoes or socks. Lindsay was a petite nineteen-year-old, and an ex-intern at the D.A.'s office, something she did two years prior when she was seventeen, but once her internship ended at the District Attorney's Office, she never stopped serving or servicing Mr. Hardy who'd hired her to clean his home whenever he thought it could use some tidying up, but she strongly suspected that the job offer was his way of staying in touch and keeping tabs on her, and since the pay was great, she went with it. It allowed her to earn some extra income and keep her head above water, the amount she earned depended on the services rendered, a proposition she thought was too good to turn down.

"Yes, Lindsay, I'll have another one—three lemon wedges and two sugars, please," he said as he stared at her breasts as they swayed back and forth each time she moved.

She turned around to go to the kitchen, and could feel his eyeballs burning a hole in her backside, she knew what to expect upon her return.

Momentarily, he returned his attention to the file before him, but instantly pushed it aside. His mind was on Lindsay, and how well her ass looked in those white shorts.

CHAPTER 38

Tensions rose drastically as the trial date neared, causing laymen and jurists alike to constantly rack their brains, speculating and publicly voicing their opinions about what they thought the outcome of the trial would be?

Vegas was thoroughly known throughout the universe for its high-stakes gambling, if the sports books inside of the casinos could have legally found a way to accept bets, whoever indulged would either lose big or win big. Several different hypotheses surrounded the hoopla, whatever the result, everyone that was fascinated by it would all find out at once. All of the spectators were full of anticipation.

Judge Mitchell Fields had never before tried or personally witnessed a trial of such magnitude, so he wanted to be sure that he had all of his ducks in a row. He went down the list, checking things off one at a time, to be certain everything was set and in place. The notices for jury duty had already been mailed to one hundred and fifty potential jurors, and one side of his courtroom was reserved for them. He'd already set aside the jury instructions he'd give this particular jury, and since the person on trial was someone they all had more than likely been taught to have high regards for, an ex-police officer, this jury would receive a special set of instructions, which would level the playing field for the prosecutor. Actually, it would probably tip the scale more in the prosecutor's favor, since a large percentage of the jury pool were possibly biased, and wanted someone to pay for the death of Shane Forbes.

Seventy-two hours before trial was scheduled to begin, all of the parties involved gathered inside of Judge Mitchell Fields' courtroom for calendar call.

"Today is the second day of October. The court is conducting a status check to be certain that everyone is ready and available on the fifth as I attempt to try what is being dubbed The Trial of The Century," said Judge Fields.

"The state is prepared to go, Your Honor," Tom Hardy said with confidence from the right side of the courtroom.

"So are we, Your Honor," said Summer Sinclair as she glanced in the direction of the prosecutor, hoping they would lock eyes, but the man didn't bother to look in her direction.

"Very well. The court is also prepared. Are there any questions before we adjourn?"

"Will the gag order still be in place, judge?" Summer asked, still looking in the direction of Tom Hardy, but again, he didn't look at her.

"Yes, the gag order still stands. I don't need any distractions from the media," the judge said. "Mr. Hardy, any questions?"

"Not at this time, judge."

"I guess it's showtime," Kevin Gaines whispered while standing next to his attorney, who had a look of nervousness spread across her face. "Baby, we can do this. We gotta do this."

Kerry came up from the audience just as her husband was speaking and saw the discomfort on her best friend's face. She didn't know which bothered her more, the fact that Summer seemed like she was afraid, or the fact that her husband had just referred to another woman as baby? It wasn't the time nor place to address the issue, so she stood next to her husband to show her support.

Summer hoped to catch up to Tom Hardy outside of the courtroom, but he was nowhere in sight when she got outside.

CHAPTER 39

Kerry and Kevin woke up in the middle of the night and engaged in some serious petting. Things had really begun to come down to the wire, the trial date was just a couple of days away, and they could figuratively feel the walls closing in on them. Intimacy would have been the farthest thing from the minds of most people in such a predicament, but for them, spooning and cuddling in the wee hours of the morning helped a lot with keeping them connected, it also reinforced their bond, especially since their future of being physically together, lay in the balance, things for them had just got real!

Kerry used the time, while Kevin was in the shower, to charge his phone. She didn't know if he'd forgotten to place it on the charger the night before, or if they'd accidentally knocked it off the nightstand during some of their rough-foreplay, but it needed some juice to its battery.

She scrolled through his list of contacts and saw a lot of familiar names, including Chief Dunlap and several more of his ex-colleagues, but one number in particular grabbed her attention. She saw Summer's number listed under *OoW*. She then pulled up the photo and saw one she thought was too provocative and very inappropriate, especially for a woman to send to her best friend's husband, which reminded her of the day before when they were all in court when she'd heard her husband refer to Summer as baby. At the time she didn't know if it was a slip of the tongue or if he was just being too friendly, and although she didn't like it, there was no way she could fathom them messing around.

She couldn't figure out why he had her listed under *OoW* or what it meant, but it compelled her to do some investigating.

She sat up in bed and quickly went to the photo gallery on his phone, and began scrolling through until she came across *OoW*. Lo and behold, she lost her breath and her heart sank. *OoW* was the acronym for *Opposite of Winter*. It was a salacious photo collection filled with nude and scantily-clad photos of Summer posing in a variety of sexual positions. *Oh my god* Kerry said to herself. She did some more digging and came across some videos in her husband's phone of Summer masturbating in different places of her home and office—she was also talking dirty and tasting herself—Kerry couldn't believe it. How could they do this to her, she asked herself? She wondered how long their secret affair had been going on, and how could they do it without her knowing about it? She wondered if Matt knew or would she have to tell him? How could her husband and best friend ultimately betray her when she'd been nothing but good to both of them? How could she ever forgive them for this? Sadly, she knew she couldn't, her mind was already made up. She wondered if Summer had damaging evidence of Kevin in her phone as well, and what other secrets they had? It didn't matter. There was nothing they could say that would make her forgive them—she felt her heart hurting inside her chest.

She climbed from the bed and went to her closet, tears streamed down both sides of her face as she quickly slipped into a pair of pants and pulled a sweater over her head, and put on a pair of running shoes, then grabbed her purse.

She was leaving in a hurry just as he came out of the bathroom, she could see that he was startled when she looked at him.

"Baby, what's wrong, where are you going?"

Kerry pointed her finger with authority as she swiped the tears from her face, then she pointed toward the bed where his phone was. "How could you and this bitch be so low, Kevin? I'm done with you."

He looked at his phone and dropped his head to his chest. He couldn't refute what he knew she saw. "Oh my god," he whispered. He wanted badly to console her, but knew he'd better keep his distance. "I'm sorry, baby."

"No, save that bullshit for them white folks when you go to court Monday. You just might be sorry when they finish with you."

There was nothing he could do but look at her, he watched as tears continued to pour freely from her eyes.

"I hope she was worth it," she whispered.

"Kerry, I'm sorry. I never meant to hurt you."

"Save it, Kevin. I promise I'm not trying to hear it."

"What about our daughter?"

"Ke'Auna and I will be fine," she said. "Come Monday, don't look for me to be in court 'cause I won't be."

Kerry was glad that he didn't attempt to stop her when she left him standing in the bedroom with only his towel wrapped around him. She reached inside her purse and grabbed the keys to the Pathfinder and left the house with a broken heart. She wanted so badly to go next door to confront Summer, but knew it wasn't worth it. Ke'Auna might already lose her dad to the criminal justice system, and she couldn't subject her to possibly losing her as well. The thought of her daughter is what kept her focused. Ke'Auna had spent the night at one of her classmates' house so she headed across town to pick her up. She wondered if there was a way to tell her what happened without making her too upset? Either way, she had to move on.

How? Where? She had no answers to either of these questions, but, in spite of that, her and Ke'Auna, together, would have to figure it out.

CHAPTER 40

Nearly three weeks after the man Summer referred to as her ace-in-the-hole suddenly resigned from his post, the criminal-minded, beautiful defense lawyer had spoken with Deputy District Attorney Tom Hardy several times on the phone, but for some odd reason, she sensed his reluctance to meet privately with her. He told her that he was in a hurry the day they saw each other in court for calendar call, and according to him, it was the reason she couldn't catch up to him afterwards. Finally, the day before the trial was set to begin, he told her with hesitance to come to his home if she wished to meet him in private.

She ascended the cement steps, one at a time, simultaneously clutching the bottom of her skirt with one hand so it wouldn't rise, thoughts racing through her mind as to what might come of the visit she worked so vigorously to get.

Her sleek black hair was wrapped neatly and pinned to her head, her all hot-pink outfit was tight in all the right places, her open-toed sandals revealed a fresh pedicure, her chiseled torso was sexy as always, and her ample cleavage looked inviting as ever.

She reached the top of the stairs and looked at her reflection in the sparkling clear glass as she approached what appeared to be the front door—she felt good about her chances when she saw her appearance in the glass, but it was the man she was coming to visit that would determine that. His approval is what mattered most, what she thought of herself didn't mean anything. She figured if he didn't like and desire what was in front of him, all of her efforts would be for nought.

Finally, she was sitting on his living room couch across from him, watching his eyes closely from the moment she laid eyes on him to see if he would check her out openly or try to be slick about it, but to her surprise, he did neither. He acted as though he was disinterested.

"Mrs. Sinclair, let's be frank," he said as he rested his head on the back of the sofa, and stared intently at the ceiling. "There's no need to sugar-coat anything, okay."

"Okay," she said, wondering where the conversation was going.

"Shooting straight from the hip, we both know why you're here and, I'm sorry, but I'm not interested," he said bluntly, purposely avoiding eye contact. "Now that that's out of the way, what else can I help you with?"

"Well, can we discuss the case?"

"There's nothing to discuss. That's what trial is for."

"Yes, but...okay," she said again, her voice dry, trying to adjust to his bluntness.

"I only agreed to meet with you because you kept insisting. I personally didn't see a need to meet with you, Mrs. Sinclair."

Summer thought of everything she did in the past to get a man's attention, she felt like she was at a disadvantage. Not once had she ever encountered a man like Tom Hardy, one who seemed to have no time to waste time, but she was determined to find his weak spot. *He has to have one—everyone does* she thought to herself. She tried uncrossing her legs to see if he'd try to get a glimpse of what was underneath her skirt, to no avail. He didn't look. She tried leaning forward to see if he would sneak a peek at her undeniable cleavage, but, again, he didn't. She then pursed her lips to see if he would show interest in her incredible salacious-looking mouth, but he showed no interest in that either. *Is this bastard gay* she wondered? He was the only man she'd ever encountered in her life who showed no interest in her. Zilch. He paid no attention to her, which was completely new to her, and something she couldn't see herself getting used to, ever! He knew himself better than anyone, so she needed him to tell her where his weakness was, because only he could.

"Mr. Hardy, it was you who told me that everyone and everything in this system is corrupt, am I right?"

"And nothing since that disclosure has changed, Mrs. Sinclair," he said, unenthused and unmoved.

"Mr. Hardy, I respect you a great deal. I really do. But, I need you to tell me what I have to do to get this case dropped against my client?"

Deputy District Attorney Tom Hardy took a moment to ponder the question. He then looked at her for the first time since she'd entered his home, leaned forward on the couch and said, "Nothing. I'm sorry."

"Tom, stop being such a dick!" she stated bluntly. "My client has lost all faith in me. He knows just like you and I that the case against him should have never been filed. Chief Dunlap pursued this because of Mayor Kason, and now that they have both resigned, this case should go away just as they have."

"It's not that simple, Mrs. Sinclair. It's a bit more complex than you make it seem," he told her. "Whatever issues you have will be resolved at trial. Again, that's what it's for. The issues you and your client have has nothing to do with me."

"Why are you being such an asshole?" she asked, looking directly at him. "Trials are a gamble. Why risk something as valuable as life with twelve strangers when a for-sure conclusion can be reached beforehand, Mr. Hardy? Mr. Gaines' wife and I are best friends, and I promised her I'd bring this shit to an end. I don't want to let her down. Please don't make me turn out to look like a fool. I'm begging you."

He seemed touched by her pleading. He appeared to soften up a bit, before looking at her with a concerned look. "Mrs. Sinclair, do you realize what I'll be risking if I order this case dropped?"

Renewed hope could be seen in her eyes as she stared back at him, she was beyond elated to see that he had finally budged. "I don't know exactly," she said honestly. "But I do know that since the mayor and chief have both called it quits, you're the only man left that can make it happen. I'll do anything, Mr. Hardy, so tell me what I can do to help with your decision?"

D.A. Tom Hardy breathed in a deep breath. He'd already told her *nothing*. Apparently he had to make himself even clearer. "Mrs. Sinclair, you've prostituted yourself to judges, police officers, prosecutors and anyone you believed you could get favors from, am I correct?"

"I do what I have to do—it's how the system works. You know that."

"I do know that, unfortunately," the D.A. stated. "Summer, you're all worn out and used up. There could be serious consequences if I do what you're asking of me. I would need something much younger and fresher to convince me. Fiftyish with plenty of wear and tear isn't going to cut it."

Summer paused as she thought about it. She was profoundly offended by his harsh, unoriginal, inconsiderate and cruel remarks, but her thoughts went to Kerry and her promise to her. The decision was not an easy one to make, but she'd come too far and was too close to achieving her goal to let her personal feelings destroy her chances. "How young are we talking, Mr. Hardy?"

"I don't know, maybe twenty or younger," he said in a perverted voice.

Summer stared at the man, looking him up and down as he sat slouched on the couch, and then tears welled up heavily in her eyes, she couldn't believe what she was about to say.

"What if I offer my fourteen-year-old daughter Heather?"

Nothing was said for quite some time. Deputy District Attorney Tom Hardy was suddenly filled with excitement. He looked over at her and said, "Call her."

CHAPTER 41

The following morning, Kevin Gaines was notified by the clerk of the court, letting him know that the trial was called off—the case against him had miraculously been dismissed. He burst into tears when he hung up. He didn't know what happened that caused the case to be dropped, but he was more than thankful. He personally thanked his attorney later on that evening as they made love at one of their secret locations. He still hadn't told her about his wife leaving, or of her discovering their messing around, her finding out was inevitable, but he decided to wait until after their rendezvous. He didn't know if the last time was the last time, so being with her again was something he anticipated.

"So, how did you finally persuade the D.A. to drop the case?" he said before kissing her shoulder.

She stared at the ceiling but didn't answer, perhaps, too embarrassed to reveal the answer. She was really ashamed of herself.

It turned out, Deputy District Attorney Tom Hardy was well hung. He damaged Heather, and made almost certain that she would never bear any children. He hoped the lineage would end—her mother was enough—additional Sinclairs were not needed, he thought.

Heather's relationship with her mom was forever ruined.

Summer and Matt's divorce was final six months after the unthinkable ordeal, and her law practice crumbled approximately two months later.

Matthew Sinclair was awarded sole custody of Heather. He was surprised to learn soon afterwards that her aspirations had changed; her dream now was to become a lawyer.

Kerry and Ke'Auna never returned home and, because of his pride, Kevin didn't bother searching for them. He and Summer also went separate ways. They wanted nothing more to do with each other.

Truth Publications LLC Presents

UNGODLY

CHAPTER 1

Fabulous Las Vegas, Nevada—also known as the city of lights, the city that never sleeps, and perhaps, its most popular tagline—Sin City. The large metropolis of Nevada has more than two million residents, and is notoriously known for attracting millions of tourists each year—gaining the reputation of being the fastest growing city on earth, the wedding capital of the world, and the gambling mecca of the universe.

The most well-known city in the Nevada desert has countless labels, but is it really as spectacular as it's thought to be? Everyone knows that it's a town that was once ruled by the Chicago mob, but also has a long history of catering to a plethora of whales and high-rollers that flock to the casinos, who are perhaps, the only ones who can truly afford to gamble and try their luck. As for the risk-takers who really can't afford to take such risks, since they fail to recognize the odds are stacked against them, unfortunately, they're forced to break the bank and are sent home. But, of course, not all can afford to get home. Some are left stranded and heartbroken, giving the city of Las Vegas the green light to tear them apart.

The desert city is known for its ruthlessness. It has more cash readily available than the U.S. Treasury, largely built by gangsters and gamblers—heavily relying on the marks who try and fail. *Marks* are the unsuspecting gamblers that the casinos prey upon. The ones who've lost all self-control, placing bet after bet, spinning wheel after wheel, rolling dice after dice, pulling arm after arm on a medley of slot machines, trying to recapture funds they've already lost, just to find themselves deeper and deeper in debt.

The city of dreams and opportunity is filled with a myriad of traps. It entices people of all cultures, from all walks of life, to travel from abroad just to visit a city they'd only seen on T.V.

The glamorous city is guaranteed to supply free alcoholic beverages to every adult who continues to gamble, hoping to boost their libidos or other agendas by surrounding them with provocative, scantily-clad women, whether it be strippers, showgirls, cocktail waitresses, keno runners, or prostitutes, and the moment an unsuspecting visitor barely crosses the line, the casinos personnel are quick to complicate their lives by calling the authorities and having them thrown in jail, instead of detaining them until they sober up then release them to go wherever they please. After all, the casinos are the enablers who contributed to the tourist's predicament—something the city's representatives will never admit to, since swindling out-of-towners out of bail and attorney money is great for the economy—something no one would dare argue against, especially those who experience it firsthand.

Las Vegas is a city that uses its big beautiful casinos and mega resorts as magnets to attract locals and people from all across the globe. The nice cars, homes, beautiful bright lights, magnificent architecture, and amazing landscapes—accentuating the flashy clothes, jewelry and expensive veneer smiles of those who stroll up and down the well-lit streets of the Strip and Downtown, could all possibly be a facade, after all, the city wasn't coined Sin City for nothing…

It's almost certain that anyone whose ever been to Las Vegas can easily come up with a few ideas of their own about why a city so glamorous and wonderfully exciting was once said to be taboo, and is still believed to be cursed, but whatever individual opinions are, whatever anyone thinks the risks and dangers are, everyone has the same thing in common—they all seek to experience the American Dream. Everyone wants to win a fortune, so they flock to Las Vegas to try their luck.

The city welcomes millions and millions of visitors each year with open arms, but the wonderful city hasn't always been this way.

The city of Las Vegas has a lot of secrets.

One of the biggest secrets is that it hasn't always been receptive to African-Americans, and no one knew this better than sixty-two-year-old Buddy Armstong—the founder and pastor of Real Love Baptist Church. He and his extremely adorable sixty-year-old wife Willa Armstrong—better known as Sister Willa, were lifelong residents of West Las Vegas. They lived on Madison Avenue, only a few blocks away from the church they built.

The Christian couple managed to stay married for over thirty-five years, but decided early on in their relationship that they had no desires to bear any children. Partly because they were both young and wild at that time in their lives—the other reason was because of the way minorities were treated.

It was the awful time in Las Vegas' history when African-Americans weren't allowed in the so called white parts of town, especially not after nightfall—they were only permitted to reside and socialize on the west side. Particularly in a neighborhood known as Berkely Square, the first housing development blacks were allowed to live, on the corner of D Street and Lake Mead Boulevard.

The west side was basically a plantation for blacks, although many were too ashamed or uneducated to view it that way.

The disadvantaged race of people were faced with circumstances of which they had no control, so accepting it and making the necessary adjustments became automatic for them, but those were the ones who wanted to survive.

Accepting conditions that were clearly unacceptable and inhumane was a part of everyday life, it was all part of what was known as the black experience.

Being limited and restricted from the so called better things in life was nothing new to the blacks who were around in that era, so they mastered making the best out of whatever they had. They realized they hadn't asked for West Las Vegas—West Las Vegas was given to them.

It was forced on them and labeled their side of town, so they made their side of town the best place to be by building and opening up black-owned and operated businesses, and watched them flourish expeditiously.

With so many hurdles, obstacles, roadblocks and bloodshed along its path, it was quite obvious to everyone within the black community that the adversary intended to watch them fail. They refused to succumb to failure and ostracism. Instead, they set out to do some amazing things.

Although more than a few perished, it was actually a beautiful and distinct time in American history when black folks actually believed in and supported each other—something that seems to be a rarity in this day and age.

Miraculously, the pastor and his wife remained close back in the day when Jesus Christ wasn't anywhere in their lives—when their relationship consisted only of sexual trysts and sin—the favorite part of their day being the Vegas nightlife.

They frequented such establishments as the historic Moulin Rouge, Love's Cocktail Lounge, The Colony Club, Sugar Hill, The People's Choice, Chances 'R', The Town Tavern, The Brown Derby, The West Side Story, Seven Seas, Elk's Lounge and, the V.F.W. Post.

The Armstrongs often rented a room at a small casino in the heart of the west side on Jackson Street known as the Cove, that was also once occupied by the late greats Sammie Davis Jr. and R&B sensation Natalie Cole.

Willa and Buddy's sexcapades developed into something much more serious once they realized they had fallen in love…

Things in Las Vegas were a lot different in those days—the city has since evolved one hundred and eighty degrees—it's now become one of the most diverse cities in the nation—blacks can now go wherever they please.

Willa Armstrong stood with one hand propped on her curvaceous hip while her well-endowed backside pressed against the dresser. "I don't like the idea not one bit," she said as she rolled her eyes, infuriated that her husband was avoiding eye contact. "There's something about it that doesn't sit well with me."

They had just gotten a visit from an old acquaintance named Lisa Miles—a drug addicted woman they once ran the streets with, who had a seventeen-year-old daughter she could no longer control.

There was a time when the Armstrongs used to drink alcohol, smoke marijuana, angel dust, and snort cocaine with Lisa on a daily basis—an activity they had long stopped indulging in since giving their life to Christ, but Lisa refused to stop self-destructing and acted as though she didn't want to shake the habit of smoking crack cocaine.

The Armstrongs could only stare in awe as their old acquaintance broke down in tears, and explained to them how impossible it had become to look after her daughter, who seemed to have lost all respect for the woman who had given her life—she apparently felt like she didn't have a mother, something she often said when she was upset.

Pastor Armstrong agreed to take her in. He knew from being around the rambunctious teen in the past that she was very intelligent and full of potential, so instead of allowing her to end up in a shelter or out on the streets as her mom suggested, he felt it was his duty as a pastor and a neighborhood leader to provide the teen with a loving home. The problem was, he took it upon himself and made the decision without first checking to see if it was okay with his wife. It wasn't, and he soon realized he'd made a mistake.

He told Lisa to have her daughter at the church at two o'clock the following day after being informed she was good at math. It piqued his interest to learn that the out-of-control teen loved working with numbers—his plan was to present her with a job offer.

Lisa Miles was ecstatic when she heard the news.

Pastor Armstrong could still visualize her excitement when she left his house, although he knew Lisa was still heavily on drugs, she didn't have the appearance of the average drug user, she was well preserved compared to other addicts he'd seen. Lisa still had the pretty-dimpled smile she was known for although her teeth could use some dentistry, he thought. Her face was the complexion of smooth almond butter and her long jet-black hair was pulled tight in a bun. The tan yoga pants she wore clung tightly to her curves, she was well endowed in all the right places, possessing a figure not even the pastor could ignore.

"Buddy, you can't just sit there and act like you don't hear me talking to you," his wife said while staring at him. "We're talking about a young girl who thinks she's grown. She's already proven herself to be very promiscuous, and you're talking about making her part of the clergy? Before you get all gung-ho, you should stop and think about how the rest of the congregation might feel about it."

Pastor Armstrong remained sitting at the foot of their bed, acting as though he was reading scriptures from his bible, pretending like he was too preoccupied to respond at the moment—one of several bad habits his wife had grown to hate.

The two had worked feverishly together to build a solid reputation that was highly favorable to Real Love Baptist Church—the most prominent church in West Las Vegas, serving a diverse congregation of nearly two thousand members.

"Sweetheart, the bible orders us not to pass judgment and to accept everyone for who they are," he finally said without looking at her, already knowing she was peering down at him. "Sometimes we have to do what's right in God's eyes, and not worry about what others might think about it."

"I understand you're a great man, Buddy," his wife began. "I also understand that it's your obligation to do God's work, but you've already done a lot of great things for this community and for the members of the church, so we have to be careful who we invite into the House of God, even when we reserve good intentions."

Pastor Armstrong shut his bible, which appeared to have been read multiple times over. "Willa, I can't believe you're passing judgment on this young child," he said in dismay. "Her upbringing has been very unfortunate, and I shouldn't have to remind you that it's not her fault."

"I'm not saying it's her fault, honey, but you can't act like it's yours or mine either," his wife retorted. "It's not our fault Lisa has chosen drugs over her own child. She should have never gotten pregnant if she wasn't prepared to take care of her responsibility. It's her job to care for Erica, not ours. We can't just sit back and let her push her burden on us."

The pastor took a few moments to reflect on his past. He knew it was only by the grace of God that he and Willa were able to escape the streets. The cocaine epidemic had swept through the black community like the plague, destroying thousands of lives in the process. He and his wife had often talked about how blessed they were, so he knew she understood how fortunate they were to have escaped its path, he found it hard to believe she was acting this way. "Baby, I don't want to get into pointing fingers, but we've all made some mistakes in life," he said before continuing. "I truly believe that if it wasn't for God showing us favor, we could both very easily still be in the streets. We were once just like Lisa, remember? We can't look down on her now just because we've cleaned up."

Willa's eyes looked like daggers as she stared at her husband, she couldn't believe he'd said such a thing. "You don't think I already know that?" she said as she moved toward him, waiving her finger in the air while awaiting an answer. "You don't need to remind me of something like that! By no means am I saying we're better than her. I know darn well I've made my share of mistakes, but what does that have to do with us coming to the rescue and taking care of a child Lisa gave birth to? It's not our fault the child turned out to be as bad as she is."

"Young Erica is just a product of the environment she grew up in," her husband replied mildly. "She's an innocent victim just like so many of our black youth. Black folks haven't always been given options. Most times we didn't have a choice, so we accepted whatever white folks were willing to give us, and most of the time they weren't willing to give us anything."

"Lisa doesn't have to keep participating in getting high, Buddy. She does it because she wants to," Willa said in a softer tone. "She had the opportunity to get out of the streets the same time we did, but since she still chooses to keep going down the same destructive path, I think we should make her suffer the consequences."

"This is about Erica, not Lisa," her husband told her.

"Regardless of the bad choices her mom made, that girl is old enough to know right from wrong, it aint no sense in us feeling sorry for her," the older woman said without blinking an eye. "She made a choice just like her mom to be out of control, we shouldn't be the ones taking responsibility for her."

"She's only doing what she knows," Pastor Armstrong said in the young girl's defense. "Her mom was not there like she should have been, so it's up to good people like you and I to intervene and do what we know is right. We have to devote some of our time to teach her what's right, and not be so quick to pass judgment on her."

"I'm not passing judgment," his wife told him. "I'm just trying to look out for the best interest of the congregation—the very people who make it possible for you and I to eat."

"That's understandable, sweetheart, and there's nothing wrong with it," her husband said in a deep voice. "We should never pass judgment on anyone. We should try our best to accept people for who they are, and appreciate them while they're still with us. We have to be careful when dealing with strangers, because we never know when we're in the presence of an angel."

"How in the world can Erica Miles be compared to an angel?" Sister Willa inquired, feeling as though he'd given a bad example.

"I'm not comparing them," her husband said. "I'm just saying we shouldn't speak ill of anyone. Whether you realize it or not, honey, you calling Erica promiscuous is passing judgment on her."

"I just don't want to have to deal with her," his wife said, truthfully.

Pastor Armstrong looked at the floor and began speaking while nodding his head. "That poor child has never had a father," he said sympathetically. "I've never understood how a man can so easily turn his back on his own children as if they're not even a part of him. To me, that's just like turning your back on your own self—God knows it's something I could never do. It's a true blessing to be able to see tiny replicas of yourself, but so many men don't appreciate it, nor do they deserve it."

Sister Willa realized it was a lost cause trying to plead with her husband. She started walking toward the bedroom door, but didn't leave the room before cleverly sliding in her final remark. "I don't give a damn what she's been through! She's not our child or our responsibility, and you shouldn't have agreed to take her in without my consent," she said before disappearing into the hallway, leaving her husband by his lonesome to wallow in guilt.

Pastor Armstrong considered retracting his invitation, but because he had already given Lisa his word, no matter how bad he began to feel or what his wife thought, he knew he had to stay strong and stick to his guns.

Books by Terrence Brothers available on Amazon

Unethical

Unethical 2

Unfair

Unfair 2

Unduly Sworn

Coming Soon Truth Publications LLC Presents

Unethical Revised

ABOUT THE AUTHOR

Terrence Brothers is a forty-seven-year-old who strives to be a professional in every aspect of the word. He is the founder and CEO of Truth Publications LLC, and even from behind bars, he's on a mission to coin the genre reality-fiction. This time he weaved together a tale about some top state officials who probably shouldn't carry the title—it is without a doubt, another page-turner.

Terrence has gone through tremendous transformation while serving at least a quarter-century in the Nevada Prison System, and he's praying that someday God will once again make him a free man. God has really been a big blessing to him, and you can best believe, he doesn't skip a beat when it comes to counting his blessings.

Terrence is a real believer, and a real trooper—he's the epitome of what it means to be tenacious. Be a blessing to Terrence by supporting him and his new company, and allow him to be a blessing to others by helping them share their stories—to say it's a win-win is an understatement.

You can contact him at:
Terrence Brothers #43397
P.O. Box 650
Indian Springs, NV 89070